THE PORPOISE OF PIRATE BAY

THE
PORPOISE
of Pirate Bay

By F. MARTIN HOWARD

Illustrated by Lynd Ward

RANDOM HOUSE · NEW YORK

To JIM HORD—

Fisherman, genial philosopher, sterling citizen, true gentleman of Nature—

This little volume is dedicated with the lasting regard of its author.

Contents

THE PORPOISE OF PIRATE BAY

FISHING IN PIRATE BAY

THE blue-green waters of Pirate Bay sparkled in the sunlight. White gulls shrilled for scraps dropped from a passing fishing boat. Then, *whoo-o-ooff!* came a blowing sound, and a sleek black creature held her round head above the water. The *whoof* was the air that had been pent up in her lungs as she dived.

W-o-o-f! came from a small black snout, as Plumpy rose beside Mother Porma. He filled his lungs with sweet air.

Just ahead, the gleaming backs of a dozen other porpoises

began to roll. They somersaulted lazily along the channel. They would blow out their breaths, almost together, then each would roll downward in a playful dive.

Plumpy himself was only about two feet long. Though no longer a baby, he was the smallest of the herd. His frisky body was streamlined, like a submarine torpedo. To the fish beneath, his little white belly must have been almost invisible in clear water. To the gray pelican gulping up a beakful of minnows, his rounded back shone like ebony.

From across the four-mile Bay, a steamboat whistled hoarsely.

At the sound, Plumpy was off with a leap of delight. The entire herd of porpoises, as usual, leveled out across the sunny stretch of water to play about the mail boat as it came steaming along the channel.

"Ho!" boomed Captain McKinley, as the porpoises boiled up at the steamer's prow. "Here's our welcoming committee."

The porpoises were cutting their best somersaults. *W-o-o-f!* Plumpy snorted, rolling and leaping ahead of the others. He began circling the boat. But the excited passengers were watching Black-Porp, the great herd-bull. Six feet of sleek dark body, moving with almost incredible speed, he led the herd.

Aboard the *Palm Scout*, leaning against her starboard railing, the captain spoke to a passenger: "One of the old ones is missing. H'mmm. I suspect some of these unlawful seine-fishermen have been experimenting with porpoise blubber. Too bad. Porpoises are harmless creatures. Very playful and intelligent. Shouldn't be killed."

Unaware of the meaning of that human talk, young Plumpy was leaping along friskily. He blew his lustiest snorts, while the *Palm Scout* churned across the Bay. Just as the passengers began to notice him, Mother Porma surged ahead. Gently she nudged him to come with her.

Plumpy turned to purl along at his mother's tail, wondering why they had left the herd.

A hundred years ago a black-flagged pirate ship had sailed in and out of these hidden waters. That was how Pirate Bay got its name. Over toward the setting sun, a swampy island had hidden the villains and their unfortunate prisoners. Snaky-rooted mangrove trees still made it a dark place. Though those human pirates had long since been hanged, other cutthroats still lurked in the darker lagoons. Huge alligators waddled through the stale-smelling mire, with bulbous eyes watching, just above tidewater, for their prey.

Mother Porma shunned this evil shore, but swam till she found a creek she knew was safe to explore. The banks of this stream were choked with palm trees and thorny vines. The in-running tide lapped against mangrove roots with a gentle, peaceful ripple.

Just ahead of Mother Porma the water suddenly began to swirl. Then, *skip! skip! splash!* Black mullet, dozens of the fat fish, leaped and fled.

The sight of those leaping fish made little Plumpy's mouth water. Until a few weeks ago, the young mammal had lived on milk, like any new-born calf. But lately he had been taught to eat fish; and this evening he felt empty with hunger.

"Come on," Mother Porma signaled, and slid forward noise-lessly. Plumpy watched, to see just how she caught the big mullet. Her bulky form glided through the water with amaz-ing speed.

The mullet began leaping high, their scaly bodies glinting like new silver. Suddenly the mother porpoise singled out the fish she wanted. She became a black streak. Though the mullet was swift, she was swifter. The fish swerved. She followed, her great snout in close pursuit. Plumpy spurted alongside to watch all that happened.

First she dipped beneath the mullet, then bolted ahead. The fish, swimming just above her flat tail, felt a powerful *wham* and shot into the air. Plumpy uttered an amazed *w-o-o-f*. As the fish, making a slow arc above the water, began dropping, Mother Porma had her mouth open to catch it.

Plumpy wiggled ecstatically, as he shared her catch. He wanted now to catch a fish for himself. But the entire school of mullet was fleeing up the winding creek.

A few moments ago Plumpy had felt a ripple of sound strike his sensitive body; a sort of scraping, stealthy sound; but he had been too interested in watching Mother Porma catch the mullet to wonder much about strange sounds. So now as Mother Porma nudged him to follow her up the creek, he felt eager to do so.

Soon the tidewater had spread till it formed a shallow bayou, fringed about with thick trees. Out in the middle of this cove

the water swirled faintly. The school of mullet had paused just there. "Now!" thought Plumpy, "I'll catch a fish for myself!"

As he pushed his round little nose out of the water to blow cautiously, he shivered with a fear he did not understand. He lowered his plump body quietly back into the water.

He had spied, half hidden in the mangrove bushes, something strange—two skiffs. In the stern of each lay a fishing net, and in the bow of each boat squatted a perspiring fisherman.

One man whispered hoarsely, "No use to put the nets out just yet. Them mullet won't hit till the tide turns out."

"Yep," said the other man in a low voice. "But reckon we'd best ease back to the creek and stretch one net across it. Keep the fish from wanderin' out o' here."

And though Plumpy the young porpoise didn't know it, wouldn't that very net pen him and Mother Porma in the dark bayou too?

PLUMPY LEARNS ABOUT NETS

THE brief tropical twilight faded. Darkness settled. The water began to turn fiery green with phosphorescence, that strange brilliance which sea water shows on dark nights.

The fisherman returned from the creek with his skiff now empty. He poled back cautiously to the other boat, and stepped in beside the other fisherman.

The tide began flowing back into the vast Gulf. Presently the fishermen softly threw one end of a net ashore. Then, very quietly, they poled the boat in a half-circle around the feeding school of mullet. Mother Porma and Plumpy had remained very still in their hiding place. Many times had the old porpoise played near fishermen. Most of the Pirate Bay crews were law-abiding and friendly, and never harmed the porpoises.

But Mother Porma felt a strange misgiving tonight about these stealthy fishermen in the hidden bayou. A shiver of memory chilled her bulky frame. Once she had seen a member of the herd trapped by a cruel fishing crew. When she herself had boiled wrathfully out of the water to help free the entangled porpoise, one of the dirty-clad men had flung a harpoon wickedly at her. It had almost struck her right in the middle of her broad black back!

But Mother Porma, crafty and swift, had somersaulted in the nick of time. Were these fishermen here tonight part of that unlawful fishing gang?

All the net was let out. The men's voices, now unguarded, cut harshly across the dark bayou. "The tide's runnin' out fast enough," grumbled one man, "but these blasted mullet still won't hit the net."

"Too busy rooting in the mud," grunted the other fisherman. He got to his feet. "I'll show you how to stir 'em up!"

His long poling-oar pounded against the bobbing skiff. The lighted lantern on its prow jumped redly, as the boat moved back and forth near the net. The men continued to pound the boat loudly.

That noise did the trick. Even Mother Porma and young

Plumpy, still under the surface, could hear the terrified mullet leap above water. Then, *zoop*, *splash*, their fleeing bodies struck the unseen net, and became entangled.

The men shouted with glee. "Guess we'll get a hundred or two of 'em now!" yelled one.

"Yep," growled the other discontentedly, "but what's a measly hundred mullet? With our whole crew, and our long seine-nets, we could pen up several acres of fish. Catch all kinds that way—mullet, trout, mackerel, reds."

"It's against the law," the other reminded him. "Some warden'll be nosin' around here pretty soon."

His partner, busy taking in his net and throwing gilled mullet into the bottom of the skiff, grunted contemptuously. "We ain't never got ketched yet—an' we shore cain't get rich *this* way!"

Mother Porma's misgivings were justified. These men did belong to that unlawful gang which lived in a hidden camp on Pirate Island. When trout and mullet schools were scarce, as they were now becoming, these men would throw together hundreds of yards of seine-nets. In this way they had swept up acres and acres of sea creatures—destroying thousands of fish they could not sell, as well as taking more than a lawful amount of food-fish.

The hidden porpoises could hear mullet flapping about helplessly in the boats. Not until the fishermen had taken in their net, and had begun poling impatiently out of the bayou, did Mother Porma nudge Plumpy to rise to the surface.

Whoo-o-ooff! W-o-o-f! sounded their long-held breaths.

Hardly had their snorts of deep relief sounded, before the fishermen stopped their skiffs to listen. "Hear that?" asked one excitedly. "Porpoises!"

The men listened for a moment. "Have a good notion to leave that net strung across the creek. We could catch them sea-hogs when they come out, an' sell their fat."

The other Pirate Islander laughed with malicious approval. "Sure! There's good money paid for porpoise oil."

But Mother Porma and her young one had already moved away. They were swimming even farther up the winding creek. Mother Porma was on the trail of more fish. Plumpy forgot the fishermen entirely, for he was again quivering with hunger.

The big porpoise halted in another cove. The water was not so deep here. Plumpy's alert senses could detect no sign of fish. He nudged his mother. Had he put his query into words, they would have been, "When do we eat again?"

Mother Porma rolled as close to the shore as possible. She threshed her powerful tail. The water churned violently. Instantly the mullet that had been hidden among the water-roots leaped and sped for deeper water.

Plumpy could see their fiery streaks through the dark water. Instinctively, he bolted after one. Up flapped his eager tail. Up, over—down came the surprised mullet! Plumpy caught it deftly in his mouth.

Ummmm! How good it tasted! Much sweeter than the big black one Mother Porma had caught before dark. These were silver mullet, smaller, but much more tender and delicious.

When they had fed until their stomachs were round and satisfied, Mother Porma nudged Plumpy. They turned back leisurely, merrily, down the creek. They soon reached the bayou where the fishermen had made their strike.

It was dark, silent. But craftily hidden under the mangroves which bordered the inlet lay the two skiffs, and across the goose-necked creek still stretched the unseen net!

All unsuspecting, Plumpy and his mother slid briskly across the bayou, and started out through the inlet. Perhaps the old porpoise was thinking about the many other things she must teach her son. Anyway, she swam hard into the net before she sensed its presence!

The great porpoise gave a mighty, swirling turn as she felt the dangerous net. Plumpy, too, had struck it. Being much smaller, he found himself slipping at once into its sagging folds!

With the swiftness of evil cunning, one of the fishermen shot his waiting boat across the creek-neck. He dragged his end of the net after him—thus completely surrounding the two fighting porpoises!

The water became a boiling cauldron of porpoise fury. Old Porma was whirling, leaping, plunging with all her mighty strength. Plumpy, too, was making a big commotion. Suddenly he found himself cut off from his mother. He was terrified.

A voice shouted above the tumult, "Go on, you frisky porpoises! Just go ahead an' roll yourselves into tangled knots. We've got you at last!"

The net was being drawn tighter and tighter. Plumpy was

now so tangled up that his chubby body was bent almost double, a most painful position for a young porpoise stuffed with fat mullet!

Desperately Mother Porma again charged the net. Her great tail was caught in a broken section of the mesh. Her furious plunges jerged the light skiffs from side to side. Their occupants yelled out in sudden consternation. "They'll sink us!" croaked one man.

"Where's my harpoon?" cried his partner, "I'll fix these sea-pigs!"

At that moment Plumpy gave a terrific lunge to straighten his cramped body. There sounded a faint snapping of old flax threads. Plumpy felt his body straighten out. He was free! He'd broken the net!

"There goes the small one!" came an angry shout.

Just then a great swelling leap from old Porma jerked the net with such fury that the skiffs cracked together loudly. Oars slithered overboard. One fisherman sprawled in his tilted boat. His partner went overboard, and reappeared, sputtering angrily.

The tangled net gave way. Mother Porma, too, was out! In anxious haste she bolted to Plumpy's trembling side. Her flat tail brushed him. "Are you all right?" she seemed to be asking.

Plumpy was all right! His *woof* of relief told her that. So happy was he to be safe at his mother's side again, that he frisked on down the creek, cutting somersaults right there in the darkened waters.

ALONE IN PIRATE BAY

DAWN was breaking over the still cool Bay when they reached it. The fiery green faded. In the air, pelicans glided low, seeking swarms of shiner-minnows. The surrounding islands lay flat and distant under thin streamers of fog. Coming to the surface, Plumpy thought the upper world had never looked so pink and wonderful; he had never felt so frisky and inquisitive.

Mother Porma turned her big nose away from the rising red sun. She felt tired. She had been on the move with her young charge for a whole day and a night, and had endured the exertion of battling a net; but she had other tricks to teach Plumpy.

The little water mammal followed alertly, wondering just what his mother was up to this time. They never slackened their brisk pace until three miles of water had slipped beneath them.

Then Mother Porma paused in the deep, indigo-blue channel of Hurricane Pass. This was a short, narrow opening which had been cut through the thinnest part of Pirate Island by a tropical hurricane. But it was so deep that a battleship might have passed through it safely.

Beyond stretched the mighty outside Gulf. Plumpy, nosing up, could see the glimmer of early sunlight on that immense sheet of green water. He had never swum out there, but he had often wondered about that mysterious world beyond his home Bay. Was Mother Porma planning to take him out there now?

Seething with wonderment, Plumpy wriggled his body just enough to keep the tide from moving him too far into the blue Pass. Suddenly he became tense with an instinctive terror. He had glimpsed a long gray shadow as it circled through the deep channel. Again he saw it, flowing through the water—a sinister bulk of pale coarse-grained skin.

A shark! For one breathless moment Plumpy was too frightened to budge. His round little body seemed entirely frozen with horror. The shark circled again. Its sharp-pointed nose turned upward—and Plumpy saw two deadly rows of close-set, bladed teeth!

The young porpoise gave a powerful flap of his flat little tail.

As if propelled from a cannon, he shot away from there.

Behind him, he could hear a violent churning of water. Plumpy spun about, terrified lest Mother Porma had been hurt by that terrible monster. A long gray body was flung out of the water. It floundered wickedly in mid-air, then fell back with a thunderous crash.

Mother Porma, wise to the ways of all the Gulf waters, had dived beneath the monster. With her powerful tail she had hurled it out of the water. She had long known how to deal with these cutthroats of the Gulf!

She rippled toward Plumpy then, just a swift dark blot. As she passed, Plumpy fell in easily at her side. They sped on together, never halting for another five miles.

As the morning wore on, a strange uneasiness stirred inside young Plumpy. Mother Porma's manner was puzzling. She seemed to be studying him, as if trying to measure just how much he had grown.

Eager to please her, Plumpy romped along beside her. He somersaulted, blew lustily whenever he needed to breathe. He brushed close beside his mother, to express his youthful affection.

Toward noon, Mother Porma halted in a place where the water was shallow and the bottom grassy and muddy.

Before Plumpy could wonder what she meant to do here, the old porpoise began circling swiftly around him. Was this a new game? Plumpy turned eagerly, and tried to circle with her.

But Mother Porma's whirling speed was too much for you... Plumpy. The water boiled turbulently. Mud began to discolor its depth. Mother Porma wriggled her great body against the soft sea-floor time and again.

The water grew cloudier and denser.

Mystified by this strange behavior of his mother, Plumpy again felt the uneasiness he had experienced earlier in the day. It was not exactly fear, but it was a strong and disturbing sensation.

Abruptly he realized that Mother Porma was no longer moving near him. The water had become so muddy that he couldn't see a foot ahead. The swirling ceased—but where was Mother Porma?

Frantically Plumpy began swimming about in search of her. Surely this was no game! Gradually the water cleared, and he knew the truth. Mother Porma was gone. Not even a distant ripple on the sunny Bay showed where she might be.

Plumpy was alone!

He shot to the surface, and blew out his breath. Surely she would hear that, and return to him! So loudly did he blow, that Plumpy himself was amazed. Why, it sounded almost as powerful as old Black-Porp!

Vaguely it began to dawn on him that he had been deserted on purpose. Some instinct deep inside him seemed to whisper reassuringly. He had grown to a stage where he must—and could—take care of himself.

Plumpy moved forward through the water. Yes, he could

take care of himself! Youthful strength and courage stirred through his muscular form. Why, he was more than just a fish. He was half-animal, too! More than that, he was, you might say, a small animated torpedo-boat! He had a triangular black rudder on his back, and one on his white underside. He had a smooth rounded nose, a streamlined body, and a flat tail that was both a rudder and a powerful weapon!

Most of all, the young porpoise had stored up in his tubular body a tireless energy that was much better than a boat's engine. He could go at will, stop at will, turn completely around in a split second. He could swim almost as fast as any fish, great or small, that swam the seven seas; and his endurance was so splendid that he could probably cruise a hundred miles without pausing for rest!

Yes, Plumpy could take care of himself!

With his old spirit of contentment and glee, he frolicked across the sparkling blue Bay. He loved the liquid pressure of clear tidewater against his smooth body. It was cool in summer, and warm enough in the mild tropic winter; just the kind of home where a young porpoise could enjoy a very happy life.

A bluish blur flitted before his eyes. Instantly Plumpy's stomach began begging. Food-fish! Plumpy shot after it. The Spanish mackerel zipped ahead. It kept just within a teasing distance of the pursuing porpoise.

All that Mother Porma had taught Plumpy about speed and fishing now came to his aid. He was suddenly beneath the mackerel. His tail lashed upward. The mackerel curved into

the air, its blue body showing bright spots of gold in the sunlight. Plumpy caught it.

How sweet and tender! He swallowed it in two gulps. He felt fine!

It was not until then that old Mother Porma, who unseen to Plumpy had followed him anxiously, grunted with satisfaction, and swam off swiftly to rejoin the porpoise herd. Her judgment had been right: Plumpy *could* now take care of himself.

A LOG THAT MOVED

UNTIL mid-afternoon Plumpy romped about the summer-bright Bay, alone but not lonely. At times he heard the *putt-putt-putt* of fishing launches. Once, rolling above water, he glimpsed the familiar plume of smoke from the *Palm Scout's* fat stack. She was far in the distance, circling toward the open Gulf on her return voyage.

Plumpy dived low, delighting in the strong pressure of deep water. His fancy was intrigued also by the great variety of salt water fish—pink trout, redfish, green needlefish, yellow jacks, gray-striped sheepshead, fragile-colored angelfish. Even the slimy-gray catfish which circled past him, goggle-eyed and with horns hanging limply, interested the wandering Plumpy.

Suddenly he noticed a brown, flat, heart-shaped creature whose body gave off a faint glow. A curiosity indeed, he decided; and he instantly gave it his full attention.

As he nosed into it gingerly, its glow became even more dazzling. But the queer thing showed no intention of darting out of his way. It simply idled there, as fearless as the young porpoise himself.

Plumpy decided he might as well teach this strange creature once and for all time that a porpoise—especially a growing bull-porpoise — must be shown proper respect. Somewhat peevishly he butted it with his snout.

Instantly an electric shock flashed through Plumpy's whole body. He had encountered his first electric fish!

Plumpy slit the water toward the surface. Up—up—out— the sea boiled as his electrified body leaped high. His prolonged *whoo-o-o-o-fff!* was a gasp of amazement.

Plumpy began to feel hungry again. It seemed that his appetite was always ravenous. As a matter of fact, the young porpoise moved about so constantly that his stomach did require a great deal of food. And eating so much gave him such energy that he simply had to keep moving!

Down along the fishing flats off Mangrove Point an unwary school of silver mullet could usually be found. Plumpy sped in that direction.

But other mullet-catchers had been there; the Pirate Island seine-crew had made a heavy strike an hour before. With hunger mounting, Plumpy hunted all over the Flats. He found nothing good to eat. He felt gaunt now. Was he going to fail so soon? Perhaps Mother Porma had turned him loose too young. Maybe—he'd starve!

He remembered how sumptuously he and Mother Porma had eaten the night before. He remembered, too, that dreadful battle with the fishing net. But just now hunger was stronger than caution. Plumpy headed quickly for one of the numerous creeks leading back into Pirate Island.

Halfway there, the young porpoise abruptly noticed a blur of blue. Was it another delicious mackerel? It was somewhat shorter and thicker. No gold spots adorned its chubby sides.

Plumpy shot forward, feeling sure it was good food for a porpoise. But as he bolted beneath it the bluefish leaped straight up. When it fell back in the water, it was headed in an entirely new direction!

Plumpy had to do some fast turning to keep the lively prize in sight. The pursued fish was much swifter than a mackerel.

Then Plumpy became impatient. He gave a burst of astonishing speed. Determinedly he crowded the fleeing fish. But again the bluefish swerved sharply. Plumpy saw its small mouth suddenly snap open and shut. Hard as bone, that curved little beak held half a dozen sharp teeth as ugly as a rattler's fangs!

When next Plumpy charged it, the bluefish gave a savage

flounce, appeared to cut a backward somersault. Next moment—coming in with the unexpectedness of an enraged bulldog—it sank its teeth viciously into Plumpy's tough hide!

Plumpy leaped in surprise. But when his sloping body lifted from the disturbed water, the sinking sun showed the bluefish still clinging vengefully to porpoise hide!

Down smashed Plumpy—down through the water he dived. Down until the grassy bottom showed itself. There he rolled frantically against the sea-floor. He was so angry he thrashed the bottom of the Bay with that stubborn little fish!

He dislodged it; but when he straightened out again, he could see nothing whatever of the bluefish. The only thing this exciting interval had done was to make Plumpy hungrier than ever. He cruised on, crestfallen.

It was gloomy in the mangrove creek which Plumpy entered. Tidewater lapped restlessly against the rooted shoreline. But somewhere close ahead Plumpy detected a faint disturbance in the water.

Silver mullet!

He came into the hidden bayou noiselessly, but determined to end his gnawing hunger. How forbidding this gloomy swamp-cove seemed! Even the water was different—less salty than the big Bay.

His attention centered on the fish near him, Plumpy planned his attack cunningly. He flashed into the small school, tail lashing upward. In a few seconds he brought three fish curving down into his ready mouth. He felt better at once, but he was still hungry. All the silvers seemed to have fled, but Plumpy's keen senses told him others would be feeding down among the hidden water-roots. He slid soundlessly toward shore.

The jungled bank was a glowering blackness. Great red mangrove roots, sheathed raggedly with oyster-shells, glimmered dimly. At one point on the bank, a rough black log protruded halfway into the brackish water.

Plumpy decided there might be fish lurking somewhere beneath that floating log. He nosed toward it. Nothing moved. No sign of fish. Plumpy paused momentarily.

To his complete amazement, the log-like thing suddenly came to life. Two bulbous green eyes shone from one end of it. The other end lashed at him like a long rough-edged knife! It was a massive-jawed alligator—far hungrier than Plumpy had ever been!

THE STRANGER ON THE "PALM SCOUT"

NEVER had Plumpy felt such fear. Never had he been so astonished. He instantly forgot his fishing. Somewhere in his brain a warning pulsed: "Swim! Swim for your life!"

Plumpy gave a desperate twist of his body. As he whirled, he felt the slashing of the alligator's vicious tail. But Plumpy had bolted out of reach. He didn't pause, but fled on across the dark lagoon.

The ugly reptile wasn't willing to give up so tempting a

meal. His steel-muscled tail lashed again. His great leathery hulk skimmed across the cove, swirling a broad wake behind him.

Already traveling fast, Plumpy now threw his streamlined body into high gear. He'd show that dull-witted old reptile a thing or two about *real* speed!

Within a very few seconds the dreadful lagoon lay far behind. The alligator gave up the race with a cough of hungry rage.

Night was upon the open Bay when Plumpy emerged from the tidewater creek. Again a greenish fire marked the liquid world below. The different fish moved about their nightly feeding, their courses sparkling like a wake of jewels.

Half a mile off shore lay smooth, sandy bottom. The water was warmer here—just the place for a long, restful snooze. It had been hours since Plumpy had rested. He felt tired, and lonely for Mother Porma. This was the first night he'd spent away from her. Perhaps even the bravest young fellow is lonely his first night away from home.

Plumpy filled his lungs with cool night air, then lowered himself to the sea-floor. Every half hour or so he glided sleepily to the surface, to blow and inhale fresh air.

When the dawn broke redly over the dew-sweetened Bay, Plumpy awoke. Sea-birds were already on the wing. Their chirping calls cheered him. At once he felt playful. He did some setting-up exercises by turning a few experimental somersaults in the water. A speckled trout leaped warily. With that, Plumpy felt immediately hungry—and so began his new day.

Soon the water ahead loomed darker, greener. It was the

steamboat channel. Plumpy's shrewd brain pictured what he hoped to find there—small blue-crusted, flat-legged crabs. His hollow insides quivered with anticipation at such a tempting vision!

He eased into the channel. The water began to ripple with life. Then—just as he'd expected—a covey of blue crabs skittered before his eyes. Their dangling, scissored claws held no menace for the hungry young porpoise. Claws were good food, too!

Plumpy smacked his lips, then he gulped down morsel after delicious morsel of the little grouches. Presently not one was left in sight.

Plumpy moved away in a swaggering roll. He'd enjoyed a handsome breakfast, and had done a good deed as well. In the future, there would be that many less crabs to tangle up the fishermen's nets.

Alive with new energy, and agog with the spirit of further adventure, Plumpy slid down the channel. A fishing boat puttered close by. Plumpy rose to the surface, somersaulted once alongside. But the fishermen, returning from an all-night job, were too sleepy and tired to notice the young porpoise.

Plumpy continued on his way. He thought of Mother Porma. He remembered the great herd with which he had loved to cavort about the Bay. They were nowhere in sight. The sun was now in the sky. Plumpy lolled at the water's surface, not certain what to do with his day.

Just then a big-beaked pelican glided within a foot or so of his rounded back, possibly thinking the porpoise was some floating bit of wreckage. Plumpy cocked his round eyes, and blew out his breath. The pelican tilted its wings in alarmed surprise, dipped almost into the water, then glided majestically on its hunting course.

Plumpy cruised off again, eager for action. At the turn of Buttonwood Island, he cut into Gulf Sound. This was a long strip of water lying between a string of small keys and Buttonwood Island. A breeze rippled its blue surface. For a moment Plumpy idled in the water, letting the vibrations play through his body. Somewhere ahead lay much activity—the throbbing of boats, the pulsing of human affairs, the mingled echoes of doings unknown to the young porpoise.

An hour later Plumpy broke water, and before him lay a small bit of land known as Gulf Zephyrs Island. It was cleared of jungle. Beaches shone whitely in the morning sunlight. Gay-colored houses, a huge hotel, stood upon that land. Many people moved about, some strolling along the beaches, some puttering about in boats.

Plumpy quivered with curiosity and a new excitement. He loved all kinds of playful activity. But instinct told him that this sort of play was not for porpoises.

Still, he rolled up close to the shore. He came up within a dozen feet of where several people were swimming. He blew a greeting, then dived so quickly they failed to see him.

"What—what was that?" asked one girl a little breathlessly.

Whoo-o-ooff! snorted Plumpy again—and the human swimmers cried out in alarm, and began stroking hard for the beach!

With a wriggle of mischievous delight, Plumpy left. A bright-colored speedboat was singing down the water. Water foamed behind it. Its prow was raised above the surface, as if trying to climb out entirely. But what speed it was making!

Here was a thing that Plumpy could do. Speed!

As the boat swept past him, his black body hurtled along beside it. The pilot, a young man with a joyous smile and considerable tan, noticed the racing porpoise, and opened up his throttle.

"Want to race me, eh? Okay, Mister Sea-pig; we'll see what you can do!"

The boat leaped ahead. It climbed gradually to forty knots an hour—speeded up until it must have been clocking off sixty miles.

Plumpy purled alongside, his blunt black nose kept just ahead of the speeding boat's high prow.[1]

"Wow!" cried the pilot with admiration. "You *can* lick my boat!" The young man toned down his roaring motor. His craft lost speed, and presently swung about in a wide circle.

Plumpy dived, and continued down the Sound. He was hungry again. The summer resort folks would have to get along without him!

Tides turned in and tides turned out. The moon rose and set. The sun, round and red and cheerful, came up at dependable intervals. Nearly a week passed thus. Plumpy continued

[1] Porpoises have been known to race low-flying planes, apparently for the fun of the race.

his trips of exploration in the waters adjoining Pirate Bay. He had gained confidence with each turn of the tide. Seldom did he go hungry for any length of time. He was indeed taking care of himself!

And then one morning, having fed agreeably on a dozen pink trout, he passed between two small keys south of the summer resort. Great flocks of birds flurried up from these small isles as the porpoise blew close to shore. They were wild rookeries, where sea-birds nested. For a few moments the air was cloudy with gulls and curlew, black geese and oyster terns.

Plumpy pressed on, more interested in the stretch of water beyond. It was not until he had glided through the margin into deeper water that he realized he was in the Outside Gulf itself!

At once his instincts whispered a warning. Young porpoises shouldn't venture into the open Gulf. Hadn't a shark almost got him once in Hurricane Pass?

With that memory came also a longing for Mother Porma and the porpoise herd. Plumpy felt suddenly very young and small, very much alone.

By noon he was cruising fleetly along the steamboat channel in Pirate Bay. Home again! Plumpy rose to the surface, and drank in a lungful of air. Even the air had a different tang to it —sweeter, more familiar, than the stale-smelling marshes, and more pleasant than the foreign scents he had detected near the summer resort.

But he could sight the herd nowhere. Had they deserted Pirate Bay? Had something dreadful happened to them?

Just then he glimpsed a familiar puff of smoke. The *Palm Scout!* Glee jerked Plumpy's body into full speed.

Ten minutes later his snout showed itself a dozen feet from the steamer's prow. Plumpy blew out his breath, and began a series of delighted rolls.

Above him on the boat stood the stalwart captain, smoky blue eyes scanning the water—just as if he were expecting the porpoise convoy.

"There's one of them," said the captain, jabbing a blunt finger toward Plumpy. "We'll probably find the herd farther along." The captain was speaking to a broad-shouldered young man who wore a khaki shirt and straight trousers. Pinned against his shirt pocket was a shiny badge. He was a game warden.

"You don't suppose any of this Pirate Island gang has been bothering them?" suggested the pleasant-faced young warden.

"Hope not," replied Captain McKinley with a slight frown. "These Bay porpoises are so friendly, I don't see why anyone should want to molest them."

The young warden looked at Plumpy, still cavorting alongside the steamer. "Porpoise blubber is valuable, you know, sir. I've had reports that some have been butchered here. When the mullet-roe season comes in next winter, and these porpoises get fat—well, these unlawful seine-crews seem to stop at nothing to make a few dollars!"

Suddenly, just before the whistle blasted its signal for the next pier, there came a widespread swirl of water near the steamer. *Whoo-o-ooff!—Whoo-o-ooff!—Whoo-o-ooff!*

It was Plumpy's lost herd blowing their greetings right and left!

"Here they are," chuckled the captain in relief. "One, two, three——" he counted them as they rolled. "No, Gregg. I don't think any of them are missing."

Plumpy began putting on a real show of water acrobatics. He leaped from one porpoise to another, as if pleading to be recognized as a member of this mighty herd.

Most of them seemed to welcome him playfully enough. They snorted lazily, flouted him with their tails. But old Black-Porp, the herd-bull, rolled along by himself. His magnificent body arched with haughtiness near the steamer's prow, as though the steamer and the porpoise herd were entirely dependent upon him to get them safely across the Bay.

The *Palm Scout* began swinging in for the salt-bleached old dock at Buttonwood Island. This was also the porpoise herd's signal to continue on their own business.

As of one accord, they suddenly swirled about, and marched off through the pleasant water in long, graceful rolls. As long as their friendly black forms could be seen, the young warden remained standing at the boat's stern rail, watching them.

They hadn't traveled far down the channel before the glossy dark bulk of old Black-Porp cut in toward Plumpy. The returned weanling found himself suddenly face to face with the great old herd-bull.

He began to feel uneasy. He wriggled his tail in the best porpoise manner of greeting. But old Black-Porp simply cocked his big, blunt head sternly, a gleam of distrust in his eyes.

"Who are *you?*" he seemed to be asking. "Do you belong to *my* band, or are you some rollicking, witless youngster from a Gulf herd come snooping into our Bay waters?"

Plumpy grew very still and tense. Didn't the herd know him? Would the old herd-bull drive him away?

BLACK-PORP LAYS DOWN THE LAW

PLUMPY rocked uncertainly in the water. He rolled slowly, blew out his breath, held it again expectantly. "Don't you recognize my voice?" he seemed to be asking of the old herd-bull.

But Black-Porp was plainly unconvinced. He continued his steadfast, critical appraisal. Plumpy racked his young brain for hint of the proper thing to do. In the old days, whenever he wanted to wheedle Mother Porma into good humor, all he had to do was brush his smooth body close to hers.

Hesitantly Plumpy slid forward. He rubbed his nose ingra-
tiatingly along the barnacle-roughened side of the old leader.

Instantly Black-Porp's mighty tail lashed out. Plumpy was
hurled half clear of the water.

Rebuked, Plumpy turned slowly about, and moved away.
Now that he'd found his beloved herd once more, he wasn't
wanted. He'd have to wander alone again.

SPLASH! Black-Porp's tail smacked the surface thunderously.

Plumpy spun about as though yanked by some unseen hand.
He didn't know why he was being rebuffed like this, but he
knew what that curt splash meant. The command to attention!

With a quiet heave of his great bulk, the old bull moved to
him. He circled the young porpoise, regarding him critically.

Plumpy quivered—not with fear, but with anxiety lest he
be rejected again. Didn't the battle-scarred old leader recognize
him? Hadn't Mother Porma contributed many a stalwart calf
to the Bay herd?

Black-Porp hadn't questioned Plumpy's identity. The old
bull, who had led his clan through many a season and many a
perilous adventure, could have detected a member of his herd
a mile away.

Lately Black-Porp had become unusually cautious. Something was brewing in the peaceful waters of Pirate Bay, something mysterious, threatening. The old bull felt it in the water,
even as alert men sense trouble in the air.

From the very day of his birth, months back in a deep, hidden
cove, Plumpy had displayed an unusual degree of restless energy

and wilfulness. So long as he was a suckling, with wise old Porma to protect him and keep him under control, he had caused Black-Porp no worry.

Today he did. As a fast-growing porpoise, Plumpy would either help the herd or he would become a hindrance to its safety. To old Black-Porp, the safety and welfare of his herd meant everything. Even a straying member, bent on some trifling adventure, might bring calamity upon them all.

Black-Porp had to be very strict about such things.

Plumpy was lying so still now he seemed hypnotized. But close observation would have shown his round eyes peering anxiously for the first sign of kindness.

With something like a grouchy grunt, Black-Porp swung around, and nosed off through the water. The whole herd turned in after him, their long smooth bodies falling in orderly line.

For a tense moment Plumpy remained fixed as he'd been left. Suddenly the voice of instinct whispered reassurance. This was also his signal to follow. He was now a member of the great porpoise herd!

And a few hundred yards away, Mother Porma herself caught that signal, and hurried to overtake them. There she had been waiting for Plumpy to make peace with the old herd-leader. For that was porpoise law: when a weanling rejoined the herd, it was no longer as a son or daughter, but as a member of the herd. And all members of that herd must abide by the rules which long experience had proved wise.

Plumpy scooted joyously through the sunny water. Quivering with pride, he frisked from one porpoise to another. His body touched them briefly, but with eloquent delight. He cavorted his way among them all, until he settled down to a steady gait just behind old Black-Porp himself.

That old master of cunning and discipline didn't seem to notice; but, from ahead, it looked very much as if he winked one shrewd eye. This lusty youngster might some day become a great herd-leader himself!

The noonday sun bore down hotter upon the Bay. The mingled smells of fish and salt tide hovered over that tropic world. The tide turned in. Shoals of fishes would presently be ranging in from outside waters. Black-Porp moved northward with his hungry family. A plan of action had formed in his crafty old brain. The herd would wait in an upper cove until the running tide brought in the schools of food-fish.

Less than a mile up that Sound, a dozen skiffs bobbed gently against the inrunning tide. Other crafty brains, too, had been scheming. Other fish-hunters—with greedier plans than the porpoise herd—were waiting. Stacked in the stern of each smelly boat was a double-length seine-net!

Uneasiness began pulsing in Black-Porp's cautious brain. He rolled on more slowly. Was that faint lapping the sound of friendly boats? Or did it mean enemies?

The subtle pulse in his brain beat steadily hotter. The herd rounded a point of land. It was not until then that the wary old herd-bull was able to get the exact range of those lurking skiffs. There were more of them than usually struck fish in one place. That much even a porpoise could tell.

And that was enough for Black-Porp. With a violent swirl he turned back upon himself. So unexpected was his about-face that Plumpy was thrown into a slanting dive.

The older members of the herd, understanding Black-Porp's action, somersaulted and headed back on their trail almost in a single motion.

As Plumpy dived, his young senses were tingling with several impressions. The water was deep in that spot, and Plumpy had sighted an enormous bulk upon the sea-floor. He couldn't tell exactly what it was. It didn't seem to be a living creature.

Much as it teased Plumpy's curiosity, he shot back to the surface. Other things too were bothering him. He *whoofed* out his breath, surprised and disappointed to find the herd turning about. Weren't they going to eat now?

Human voices reached him faintly. The watchful array of seine-fishermen had spied the porpoises. Dimly, Plumpy seemed to recognize the harsh sounds they uttered.

But before he could wonder about it, sudden power heaved up beneath him. Plumpy felt himself hurled high. When he hit the water a second later, he was headed properly after the disappearing herd. Black-Porp's stern snout had got him going!

A thousand yards down the Sound, a black, closely weaving shoal of mullet halted. They had just arrived in the Sound, ranging in from the outside waters. They sensed the approach of porpoises. Excitedly the immense school changed its course Instead of moving up East Sound, it fled down the long reach of Pirate Bay. On down the Sound came Black-Porp's hungry family, only to find that the fish had eluded them.

And behind the porpoise herd, the Pirate Island seine-crew was giving vent to a terrible wrath. They were so angry that their light boats bobbed madly under their heavy feet.

"Them blasted porpoises have scared the mullet away from the Sound. I'm going to make blubber-lard outta them crafty old sea-hogs one o' these days!"

Thus the unlawful fishermen had cheated the porpoise family out of its meal—but the porpoises in turn had saved the large school of mullet from those lengthy seine-nets.

A SERIOUS MISTAKE

BY another long turn of the moon, Plumpy decided he was established as a full-fledged member of the great black herd. Alert to every movement of the porpoise family, he tried to conduct himself agreeably. His frisky spirit, however, remained at a high pitch, as did his irrepressible eagerness. Day by day he learned new methods of fishing from the crafty old herd-bull. He learned, too, to wait for Black-Porp's signals.

It was in the brief tropic twilight, following a golden-bright afternoon. Plumpy's herd had chased a shoal of mud-mullet for over a mile, but the tide was running out fast. The mullet, anxious to reach deeper water anyway, fled into the open Gulf.

Black-Porp suddenly turned the backs of his family to the setting sun. He led them purposefully down the full length of the Bay. Plumpy's instincts had grown miraculously keen these past few weeks. They told him now that somewhere, perhaps not very much farther on, he and his band were to dine on toothsome fare. He couldn't guess what it would be, but he began to feel that a thrilling experience lay just ahead.

As usual, Plumpy was traveling well in the front ranks, for the young fellow had grown rapidly. As they approached the east point of Seagrape Island, Black-Porp veered slightly to port. Presently he halted his family noiselessly.

Plumpy tested the faint vibrations in the water. The tide had ebbed to a standstill. It would be turning in again within another minute or so. Again that subtle premonition of a new and thrilling experience stirred Plumpy's senses.

What was it they were after this evening? What kind of delectable fish were they to feed on? The herd had traveled miles. Plumpy was becoming keenly interested in eating!

Black-Porp forged ahead, reassured. So pleased was Plumpy, so filled with hungry expectancy, that he nosed his sleek body still farther ahead. Almost before he knew it, he was rolling along soundlessly, shoulder to shoulder with the old herd-bull himself.

Black-Porp didn't seem to mind, or, for that matter, to notice. The old leader's attention was focused intently on something which stirred faintly. Plumpy himself tried to course the mysterious vibrations. They seemed to come from the lea of the distant lighthouse on Seagrape Island.

Black-Porp began circling, heading for the deeper Gulf-tide which turned in at the tip of the island. A half-mile of water slid past them. Another half; another quarter. Then——

Black-Porp paused for a moment, then slid on again with increased caution.

Plumpy was seething with excitement. This "feeding feel" inside him was different. The water vibrations he felt were different from those made by mullet or trout, or even gold-spotted mackerel.

When another hundred rolls were made, the leathery old herd-bull veered away from the lighthouse. Schooled in all the strange ways of the sea, he meant to circle that unseen shoal of fish, cut them away from the outside deep.

Plumpy had had no experience with the deer-like wariness of this new species of fish. He knew only that they were close by.

The weaving motion telegraphed through the water grew more readable. Plumpy could even tell that these were not long slender fish, but were oval-shaped and flat.

The yellow beam of the lighthouse cut its slow circle. Plumpy glimpsed a leaping body. It looked like a blob of molten gold!

That was too much for Plumpy. His suppressed eagerness, his sharpened senses, his gnawing appetite all urged him forward. The tricky glimpse of golden food set him off as a flash sets off dry powder. With a soundless explosion of muscular

speed, he charged straight toward the shoal of golds!

The golds, detecting this sudden torpedo-like approach, came to suspicious attention. It all happened in a trice, then. Plumpy's form came among them like a dark projectile.

Instantly, hundreds of flat, oval-shaped fish leaped into the air. Fine-scaled bodies shone fleetingly like clean rose-gold. The whole school of pompano—that choicest of all sea-foods—retreated in haste to the open Gulf!

Black-Porp, a hundred yards away, heard it all. His outraged form hurtled toward the fleeing fish, trying to head them off. He arrived as the very last of the pompanos skipped through the broad pass.

Behind him rolled his disappointed herd. Their *whoo-o-ooffs* broke above the water, the voicing of double disappointment. Nor had Plumpy himself got one morsel of the food!

Plumpy rolled uncertainly back toward the herd, looking somewhat like a headstrong puppy returned from chasing a cat. He felt crestfallen, and uneasiness began to disturb him. He'd fumbled this catch—had made all the porpoises miss their needed meal.

Black-Porp came bolting. Rage for the disappointment of his herd gleamed in his deep-set eyes. Plumpy took refuge in the midst of the idling porpoises. That was an old reaction of his babyhood—to seek protection from anything among the oldsters. But the herdlings parted quickly away from him. The laws of the porpoise herd are definite. Black-Porp came in, his visage in the darkness glowering sternly.

The only prompting Plumpy felt just then was one for speed. He realized, all in a second's time, that he had committed a grave error. He'd have to pursue his life again, alone and on his own—and he'd have to start pursuing it right now!

His sleek body shot up the Bay, marking a foaming trail through the phosphorescent tide. Black-Porp, grunting into a tremendous burst of speed, tried to overtake him. He couldn't. For flowing ceaselessly in Plumpy's young body was a strength and speed perhaps never possessed by another porpoise! Plumpy was already a half mile away, still traveling like black lightning.

The main herd idled where it lay. The old bull hove too, water swirling violently about his great body. He refilled his lungs with cool night air, trying to cool his angry brain. He felt tired, and again his recent worries returned to him.

The seine-skiffs which his family had encountered more and more often nowadays whispered a strange warning to the seasoned old leader. The feeling was strong upon him that Plumpy had no business wandering around the Bay by himself.

Black-Porp splashed a signal with his tail. The rearward herd flowed into rolling advance. When they arrived, Black-Porp pressed forward, uttering a grouchy grunt that carried a hint of age and weariness.

The herd moved along in Plumpy's vanishing wake.

THE GREAT SILVERY CLAN

A LEAGUE and a half up the Bay, Plumpy slackened his speed. He didn't feel a bit tired, but his cheerful spirit had somehow deserted him. Instinctively he felt like an outcast. Such a feeling was disturbing; for lately the fast-growing porpoise had dimly sensed his destiny—the destiny of a great herd-leader.

An outcast, a lone wanderer, could hardly become the leader of a mighty herd!

Plumpy turned in among a ragged group of tiny islands. Here

the sea-floor was grassy, and he found enough food to ease his gnawing hunger.

He passed the night in a remote part of the Bay, but he found little excitement. There were no kindred spirits to frolic with him. It seemed that every creature that moved by night in the water was intent upon but one thing, the necessity of getting something to eat.

Stars laced the heavens. They were reflected by the tranquil Bay. The high moon, a sickle of silver tonight, cut across the sky. The water lay still. The mysterious silence was broken only by the occasional deep grunting of a drumfish, or the distant crazy laughter of an island loon.

When the first day-bird began to stir on its jungle roost, Plumpy was glad to come out of his retreat. How lonely he'd been all night!

Darkness still hovered over the Bay. The sun hadn't yet risen. But Plumpy knew, as the awakening birds knew, that another day was dawning.

He could never resist the call of adventure when a new day began. He boiled along through the water, threshing his flat tail, and blowing out his breath in gusty *whoofs*. He was trying to splash up a bit of cheer in the quiet of early morning.

Suddenly, roving up from out of the rising sun itself, it seemed, appeared a tremendous horde of great fish. What strange band was this?

A half-thousand bright-scaled creatures, each almost as large as a grown porpoise, were making for Hurricane Pass. How gracefully they swam! How majestic they looked! Never had Plumpy beheld such a mighty clan.

He dived low, seething with curiosity. Were these food-fish? Or were they enemies? Plumpy's instincts rejected both possibilities. True, they appeared somewhat like overgrown silver mullet. But——

Water, red-gold under the risen sun, curled and trailed back in a broad wake. The mysterious horde seemed in no hurry. They rocked and rolled and dived and sliced the water sportively, very much as Plumpy's playful herd loved to do.

But Plumpy heard no *whoofs* of breath come from these enormous creatures. They were not smooth-skinned mammals, but scaly fish.

From underneath, Plumpy studied them in round-eyed admiration. Their long, graceful forms glinted bright as silver in the blue-green water. How happy they seemed!

Plumpy, the lone wanderer, felt suddenly homesick for his own great herd. But he was still afraid to face the wrath of old Black-Porp.

A curious urge suddenly pulsed in his young porpoise brain. Perhaps he could join this mighty band of friendly-seeming silver folk!

Plumpy shot forward, fascinated by that idea. He came up, up, up—and blew out his most impressive *whoof* in the very midst of them, a sleek black pigfish in the midst of flashing silver tarpon! Now, if these magnificent Silver Kings would only accept his offer to become one of them——

Instead, two dozen shining bodies were instantly leaping high in surprise. The sun struck their bodies with a clean glitter. Arched backs were of a sea-green cast.

Other tarpon began to leap. Was this their manner of greeting?

A tumultuous, deafening commotion took place. Aware now of an uninvited alien in their midst, the proud tarpon clan went into violent action—in front, on both sides, to the rear of Plumpy!

Incredible numbers of arched backs clove the early daylight in resentful arcs of flashing silver.

Plumpy was terrified by this unexpected reception. One after another, those powerful bodies surged up beneath him. Higher and higher he was lifted. As he fell each time, other arched backs were instantly beneath him, passing him up into the air again!

Plumpy felt outraged. This was certainly no way for a porpoise to be treated!

Onward rolled the endless ranks, swiftly, violently. In a frenzy of panic Plumpy felt himself whirling over and over. He tried to dive. Dozens of other tarpon seemed to be just beneath him. He was toppled and jostled until his vision became a weird blur of shooting forms, glassy round eyes, and upturned, bone-hard noses!

Plainly, the proud Silver Kings meant to have no porpoise among them! Plumpy felt a flame of indignation burning within him, but for once he was powerless.

The last score of the trailing horde broke under him. For a few seconds Plumpy reeled along in their turbulent wake. Then he sliced the water with a burst of fury, aiming for the surface. But he was so confused that he buried his snout in the muddy sea-floor instead!

Glug-gurgle. His grunt of surprise bubbled up to the surface. With a wrathful twist of his body, Plumpy righted himself, and shot up.

The tarpon horde was now churning through the deep blue of Hurricane Pass. Plumpy gave them no more attention. With a disdainful lash of his tail, he catapulted through the water, bound in a straight course down the Bay.

Whew! What an experience!

THE DEMON OF THE SUNKEN GALLEON

WITH such speed did Plumpy move that he had traversed three leagues of Bay water before the tarpon horde had played beyond Hurricane Pass. Let them go their own way, he would go his alone!

He cut through the very center of a migrating string of red snappers, and plowed on through the lower end of Pirate Bay. He was halfway up East Sound before he realized where he was going.

He halted to let the various signals of the deep play through his senses. The tide was turning in from the Gulf. Fish would be moving in presently. But just now Plumpy could detect no approaching shoal.

He moved ahead.

The sun had disappeared behind a bank of clouds. A Gulf wind was blowing gustily up the Sound. Rain began to pelt against the choppy water.

Plumpy felt his recent indignation cooling. He swam along the surface, tingling with pleasure as raindrops pattered against his thick-skinned back.

But as the waves grew in size, and began to show foamy crests, the porpoise dived. Down below, the water was scarcely rougher than usual, but the cloudy sky darkened its transparent green. Faintly Plumpy could hear the steady drizzle of rain against the surface.

It was then, as he passed into the old ship's channel no longer frequented by large vessels, that Plumpy realized why he had cruised down the Bay and entered East Sound.

Dimly in his senses had pulsed a memory of something he had seen that day when the unlawful seine-crew had turned old Black-Porp's herd back down the Sound. The fascination of that mysterious hulk had grown in Plumpy's memory until it was now almost a visible question mark before his eyes!

Chased away by the old herd-bull, and his friendliness spurned by the tarpon, Plumpy felt in just the mood for a thrilling adventure today. Since it was rainy and rough at the water's surface, he might as well remain down under and occupy part of his time exploring!

A dozen body-wriggles below, Plumpy sighted that strange bulk. It appeared darker and gloomier this time. Plumpy knew it was no living thing; but, even as he nosed closer, a shiver of uneasiness passed through his frame. What was this dark body lying half submerged in the mud at the bottom of the Sound?

Plumpy couldn't know it, of course, but this was the hull of a sunken ship. It might be the same pirate sloop sunk by government battleships a hundred years ago, after the evil buccaneers were hanged from their own yard-arm!

It was a ghostly-looking thing to Plumpy. A green scummy moss gave it a slimy appearance. Plumpy scouted around it, goggle-eyed. What monster of the sea claimed it now? The mid-cabin yawned open in watery gloom.

Plumpy swung in toward the waterlogged stern. No fish swam here. Perhaps there was nothing of interest to be found, after all.

But just then he noticed a half dozen odd-shaped little creatures dangling before his eyes. Jellyfish? No, decided Plumpy; these small things were yellowish-gray. Their bodies looked like tiny globes, and their numerous legs wavered in the water like elastic bands.

Were they good to eat? Snapper, mullet, jellyfish—Plumpy already had such a mixture of food in his stomach that perhaps one more kind couldn't hurt.

With a sudden rush he guzzled one of the dangling bits of

flesh. *Ummmm!* Plumpy's eyes fairly bulged in surprise. That was about the sweetest morsel of food he'd ever sampled.

He promptly tried another. This time he had to chase it toward the yawning, water-filled boat cabin. It was just as toothsome, a real porpoise delicacy.

He looked about for a third. But the rest of them seemed to have vanished. Plumpy thrust his snout boldly into the cabin-door.

The dark green water inside revealed nothing for a moment, but suddenly there was a slight trembling from the shadowy inner depths. Plumpy quivered in sudden panic. He had a glimpse of long, suction-cupped arms dangling loosely.

Next instant a large globe-pot of a body, which looked for all the world like a huge grinning death's-head, lunged toward the porpoise at the slimy threshold!

A shudder of horror convulsed Plumpy's body. With greedy eyes bulging, the ghostly monster moved forward!

Plumpy swirled, and the water seethed with soundless violence. The terrified porpoise made for the surface in one long frantic lunge. He had been feeding on baby octopuses, and the gigantic mother had suddenly appeared, to make a meal of him.

But Plumpy had moved too swiftly. He broke water, and still shuddering at the horrible monster lurking somewhere down there below him, he swam rapidly on down the channel.

How he longed for his herd! The porpoise is not a solitary creature by nature. Plumpy wanted other porpoises to play with. He liked pitting his own cleverness and speed against theirs. But he passed two more lonely days and nights without gaining the faintest sight of the herd. Perhaps his own helter-skelter movements were to blame. He cruised up and down the long Bay, ducking in and out of tidewater creeks, but nowhere could he find a trace of the big black herd.

Plumpy didn't know it, but old Black-Porp had led the herd up a river that reached into the Florida mainland. Far up that great stream was a beautiful winter resort for human creatures. Across the river there, stretched a high cement bridge, and Black-Porp loved to frisk about near it, while people above looked down at the porpoises with cries of admiration.

ANOTHER MEETING WITH AN OLD FRIEND

PLUMPY remained a lone wanderer for another week. It was a rainy week, too, and the young fellow became fretful.

Most of the time he was able to find sufficient food. One day, however, shifting schools of fish kept him hustling to get anything at all to eat, and the day after that his plight became serious. He finally ventured into the hidden fishing flats along Pirate Island. A reef of mangrove-covered keys hid the section from the open Bay.

Plumpy had detected the presence of fish shoals. But when

he nosed cautiously into that water, he found something very different.

The Pirate Island seine-crew, a dozen men with dirty nets in a dozen skiffs, were making an unlawful catch!

Plumpy's view of this was incomplete, and he understood little of what he saw. But he was instinctively wary of so many fishing boats in one place.

The dozen long seines were locked together in an immense circle. That circle, marked by a continuing line of bobbing corks, was already closed around many thousands of fish. The fishermen were laughing with gleeful triumph. "Bet we got fifteen thousand pounds," gloated one.

"We got to hurry an' make 'em hit the nets," spoke another fisherman impatiently. "We'll have to clear out o' here before some fishwarden comes nosin' into our business!"

Plumpy dared not venture closer. He could hear the men clattering their poling-oars against the boats. The penned fish, frightened, struck the gill-nets a hundred at a time. Their frantic splashings were plain to the submerged porpoise. His empty stomach pinched at the sound of so many fish—but he was too cautious to stay. He turned soundlessly back into the open Bay.

Meanwhile, the fishermen were pulling in their long nets. They ungilled thousands of mullet and trout. They threw back into the water thousands of other fish which they could not use, but many of these were bleeding, their gills so torn by the nets that they died.

For hours afterward, Plumpy found no fish anywhere. This tremendous net-strike had telegraphed its warning throughout the surrounding waters. Other fish fled to the outside Gulf, where Plumpy dared not venture.

The young porpoise was both hungry and lonely. No herd. No food. Nothing but empty water and a gloomy sky above it!

Dejectedly he cruised down the entire length of the Bay, and was finally rewarded with a generous meal of mullet which he found in the shallow waters of a muddy creek. He felt like frolicking now, but nowhere could he find his herd.

He cruised back up the Bay. Suddenly he halted, senses alert with rekindled hope. A distant but familiar vibration flickered through the tide. Plumpy lay tense, straining to unravel this mysterious signal.

It came again—the far-sent vibrations of smooth-rolling bodies. The porpoise herd!

But just then he heard still another sound. *Pomp-pomp-pomp—pomp-pomp-pomp*——

Plumpy *whooshed* to the surface, surveying the choppy waters in all directions. Down he dived again, his senses keyed to a wistful, anxious pitch.

He couldn't quite find the trail of his herd—but he suddenly recognized that other, much different, sound. It was the diesel-motored fishing boat, which was now running down the channel. Plumpy, rising again to the surface, could see it clearly. It was a forty-foot craft which he had watched many times before. It came to Pirate Bay twice a week to collect the food-fish placed in outlying ice-houses by friendly and law-abiding fishermen.

To the young porpoise, that throbbing diesel boat was a welcome distraction. With a delighted flout of his tail he rolled toward it.

Two men stood at the low rail amidships. One of them was Warden Gregg, the same young man who had stood on the *Palm Scout's* higher deck. Beside him was the fishing boat Captain.

"I've been tipped off," remarked Warden Gregg, "that this Pirate Island seine-crew is striking again. Too lazy to use lawful gill-nets, they're ruining the future fishing business in this Bay for our hard-working men."

The Captain shoved his cap over one ear, and scanned the distant shores of Pirate Island. "Yep. It's likely true—but ye'll have a hard time ever catchin' them blighters. Sharp, they are. Modern fish-pirates!"

Plumpy boiled up out of the water just then with a lusty *whoof* of greeting.

Warden Gregg's youthful face crinkled into a smile as he saw the frolicsome porpoise. Then a frown crossed his face. "Captain, this young fellow is cruising by himself again. Why doesn't he keep with his herd?"

"Young, an' got the wanderlust, I reckon," chuckled the grizzled Captain. "Guess the main herd is feedin' somewhere nearby."

Plumpy flipped a double somersault through the water. *"Whoo-o-ooff* — how's that one?" he seemed to ask, with a wriggle.

"You'd better romp on back to your herd!" called Warden Gregg. "First thing you know, these greedy seiners will have your carcass stripped for porpoise blubber!"

BATTLING A KILLER

AT the margin of a grassy shallow Black-Porp hove to with his herd. He had traveled all the way down the river with his family. They were ready to dine—if they could catch something to eat.

Every instinct of the experienced food-finder jerked the old herd-bull suddenly alert. Fish shoals ahead!

But though he quickly recognized the proximity of mullet, Black-Porp remained strangely still. He was listening to other vibrations, even as the telltale signals of weaving mullet grew

stronger. The battle-scarred old bull moved his herd resolutely ahead.

More and more distinct, too, grew those other watery signals. Black-Porp again halted cautiously. He discovered the mullet school's precise location—a slight nose-turn to the right. And just then he recognized the meaning of those other vibrations—the faint, challenging approach of danger!

Some other enemy of the mullet was driving them toward the porpoise herd. Water trembled ahead. Bright-glinting bellies now marked the sun-struck ceiling a few lengths away. Black-Porp knew that his hungry herd must take this chance. He touched off his mysterious signal. The porpoises charged into the living shoal of food, and at that very instant the enemy on the other side of the mullet school did the same thing.

It came threshing into their midst without care or mercy—a ten-foot, sandy gray monster. Fully four feet of that length was a protruding bony beak set closely with sharp two-inch teeth.

Sawfish!

The mullet school spread in a horrified frenzy. Already a score of them were hacked into ragged fragments, and floated along the surface, trailing crimson streaks.

Black-Porp halted in a swelling rage. He knew the fierce savagery of the sawfish. Slayer of a dozen times more fish than it can bolt down its greedy gullet, the monster takes vicious delight in slashing into any creature foolhardy enough to fall within range of its deadly blade. Even great whales have been known to receive fatal gashes from the sawfish's butchering weapon!

The mullet had vanished, but on came the threshing sawfish. Black-Porp smacked out a command to his herd. One jab of that spiked weapon could lay open their plump sides. The mothers and yearlings fell back, and the old herd-bull faced the menace alone.

Thus it was that Plumpy, rolling up with a wriggle of delight at sight of his long-lost herd, found them all tense with apprehension. His senses were immediately sharpened. At sight of Black-Porp facing the battle alone, some instinct of loyalty pulsed hotly in Plumpy's brain.

His young muscles were strong, like supple steel. Heedlessly he shot forward to old Black-Porp's side. But Black-Porp hurled him back into the safety of the herd. When Plumpy, giddy with astonishment, righted himself, the old herd-bull had disappeared.

What was going to happen?

At that moment a thing of fury exploded beneath the sawfish, whose coarse-skinned body was hurled clear of the water. Old Black-Porp had struck first!

The sawfish buckled wickedly in mid-air. Falling back, he aimed his deadly weapon for the porpoise bull's flank.

There was a whisk of air, a loud slicing of water, as the spiked blade plunged downward. But Black-Porp, side-slipping with incredible agility, wasn't there!

Again there came a furious upsurge beneath the killer-fish.

As he fell back to the water this time, his saw teetered edgewise, pointed below, and slashed again at the old porpoise.

The whole herd milled about in sudden agitation, for it seemed that their courageous old leader had been punctured. But Black-Porp reappeared. Only a faint streak of red showed slantwise along his stern. He had dodged in the nick of time!

The killer-fish sought to bore in closer to the main herd, but again and again Black-Porp smacked him into the air.

Suddenly the sawfish slithered past the old bull's guard and charged furiously into the non-fighting young porpoises!

Black-Porp's great mouth flew open. Two rows of small, close-set teeth clamped firmly upon the killer's leathery tail. With a violent lunge that shattered the water for twenty feet around, Black-Porp tugged the sawfish backward. A second later he heaved him high in the air!

Grunts of savage outrage now drummed inside the monster's floundering hulk. Black-Porp himself blew out a weary snort of breath. The porpoise family was again milling about anxiously. They sensed that their leader was tiring.

Plumpy forgot the old bull's signal to stay out of the fight. Young fury grew in him as he saw the killer-fish battering down the courageous veteran.

Plumpy dived deep. He came up with unerring accuracy right under the sawfish and forced all his young strength into one sudden effort. Brilliant light and garish darkness sprayed through his brain at the terrific jolt! Luckily Black-Porp had heaved at the same instant. Their combined strength was a telling stroke.

It turned the battle. The sawfish fell back to the water, stunned. Its rough tail quivered helplessly.

This was the herd's cue, the cue they'd been anxiously awaiting. They rushed in. All sensed that they must complete this dangerous work at once.

Half a mile distant glinted a sheer white bank of sea-shells. They had been thrown there many centuries ago by some early race of man. The water was deep along that bank. Beyond the jagged shell-bank lay the jungle, broiling hot under the tropic sun.

With a grunt of disgust for the carcass of the sawfish, Black-Porp took a firm tooth-hold on it. He began shoving. The lifeless killer-fish was moved slowly but with grim resolution toward the distant shell-bank.

The herd rolled along in this strange wake. What was Black-Porp doing, wondered Plumpy. He purled forward inquisitively. He had helped conquer this sea-enemy. Shouldn't he have a part in this strange work, too?

The leader's great mouth was too full to offer any resentment. Plumpy nosed in and clamped his own jaws helpfully upon the hated carcass.

Thus the strange parade continued, Plumpy shoving from one side, the old herd-bull pushing from the opposite. They reached the shell-bank. With a mighty heave Black-Porp bolted the heavy body from the water. It caught on the jagged shells and stayed there.

The evil spiked blade would bleach in the hot sun. From

over the jungle, bald-headed vultures would circle toward it—
closer, ever closer——

The pleasant Bay waters would no longer be polluted with
that savage killer-fish!

A NEW BOAT IN PIRATE BAY

TROPIC summer burned its course over Pirate Bay. Always the tides flowed in and ebbed back into the mysterious Gulf. Sometimes sudden squalls struck the Bay with brief fury. When they did, cotton-crested waves sent the porpoise family into deep retreats.

Plumpy grew amazingly. Throughout this period he had stayed with the herd. He had roved with them, fed with them, frolicked and prospered with them. His tubular body had grown to four feet of sleek muscle and incredible speed.

Old Black-Porp's worries had increased his cautiousness. He still sensed trouble brewing, and he seemed to grow grumpier with every swing of the tide.

The herd was feeding one day through the shoals of Gulf Sound. Plumpy had lost nothing of his frolicsome spirit. He was rolling in play with one of the yearling porpoises. Time after time they matched their lusty young strength, as might two cattle yearlings in the woods. They would brush their rounded noses together, then each would try to heave the other out of the water. Though Plumpy had grown astonishingly fast, he was still smaller than the yearlings. But a second after he touched noses with his opponent, he was beneath him. The other porpoise found himself catapulted through the water with surprising force.

The yearling porpoise didn't seem to mind. Like Plumpy, he was very good-natured. He righted himself, and immediately engaged his younger herd-mate in another set-to. Plumpy obliged, and once more sent the porpoise tumbling across the surface.

Another porpoise yearling appeared. He rolled toward the frolicking Plumpy with a gleam of determination in his pig-like eyes. Plumpy awaited him. His tail twitched expectantly.

Without going through with the ceremony of brushing noses, this new opponent, a good ten inches longer, heaved up and swept Plumpy into the air!

Plumpy grunted with surprise. He wasn't hurt, for his compact body was as elastic as a hard rubber ball, but he didn't mean to let this larger fellow get away with such tactics!

Next time Plumpy foiled the other's sly attempt to dart under him before touching snouts. As he cut downward, Plumpy dropped with him. Down, down—Plumpy forced his body alongside the other. His opponent blew a chain of disgruntled bubbles toward the green ceiling of water. But Plumpy resolutely rubbed jowls with him, then, quick as black lightning, exploded his powerful strength under the other's white belly.

As the incredulous porpoise tumbled along the Bay surface, Plumpy waggled around him watchfully. His manner showed only the friskiness of good fun. Neither of the frolicking youngsters noticed old Black-Porp eyeing them.

Plumpy's larger playmate slid past his guard. A second later, Plumpy felt small teeth clamp about his tail-paddle! He was shaken vigorously. The other porpoise seemed to resent the superior strength of a younger and smaller herdling.

Anger swept through Plumpy's brain. This wasn't play. He wouldn't stand for it! His paddle was his rudder as well as his instrument for catching food.

For the next two minutes Plumpy's tireless young body marked a swift dark pattern of spirals, lunges, and bucking heaves, as he pummelled his resentful playmate.

Black-Porp's mightier tail smashed a signal against the water. Neither heard it, and the old herd-bull charged in between them, and hurled them in opposite directions.

The rowdy tussle ceased. Lately the old herd-bull wouldn't

tolerate too much splashing in one spot of the Bay. He was growing more and more cautious.

An unfamiliar noise came down the Sound. The porpoises heard it. Plumpy came to attention himself. So this was the reason why Black-Porp had silenced their play!

A thirty-foot fishing launch was crawling toward them. It was a new boat, with white gunwales sloping low to the water.

Plumpy scudded forward a few rolls, curiosity burning in him. He hadn't seen this new craft before. Was it a friendly boat? Perhaps the men, concealed in the canvas-covered steering compartment, would cheer the porpoises, as the *Palm Scout's* passengers always did.

A signal halted Plumpy. It was barely audible, but Plumpy knew the old herd-bull had ordered him back. He swirled around instantly.

What was wrong? Already the main herd had submerged. Plumpy dived, too, and overtook them. With scarcely a visible ripple, Black-Porp led his family away.

Two days later the porpoise family was roving the upper reaches of the Bay. The water was rough today, and the whole herd had to snout up their food from low mud-flats.

Plumpy hadn't seen the strange motor launch again, but memory of it had stayed in his senses. He was also still curious.

A late summer thunder squall broke over the Bay. At such times it was Black-Porp's custom to retreat with his herd to the deeper water of some inland bayou where the land might keep the rougher storm back. They moved in that direction now.

Plumpy was outermost on the starboard flank of the retreating herd. The herd-bull lay some dozen rolls to port.

In a way, Plumpy thrilled to these brief but violent squalls. He enjoyed pitting his strength against the agitated undertow of the waters. He loved, too, the fishy smells which the turbulent water brought to him. And there was always that mysterious song of the vast Gulf wavering through the tide at such times —an exciting, luring song, which Plumpy couldn't quite understand.

Close ashore, Plumpy ruddered upward, and discharged his breath into the storm. Wind whistled through the long fringe of jungle. Very dim in the darkening storm, Plumpy glimpsed the strange motorboat! She was riding the breakers gracefully, headed steadily for some channeled creek winding back into Pirate Island.

At that moment Plumpy's instincts were in conflict. The herd had moved on, seeking its storm shelter. But the luring whine of the Gulf was strong in the water, and yonder, several hundred rods distant, was the new white boat.

Plumpy decided he must *whoof* alongside the boat just once. He set a straight course for the storm-rocked boat.

Aboard the fishing launch were huddled half a dozen men. "This is the sort of boat we've been needin'," remarked one man. "She's fast, an' she's seaworthy."

The others grinned crookedly.

"We've already paid for her, from these heavy seine-strikes

we've been makin'. Guess we can clean out all the fish in Pirate Bay now!"

"Yep," agreed the rough-bearded pilot with a sly grin; "an' don't forget we're goin' to clean up that porpoise herd just as soon as roe-season comes in. We can make a tidy sum of money on their blubber-oil!"

PLUMPY TAKES TO THE AIR

THE new launch bore the name *Bay-Rovers* on her jumping prow. She waded out of the squall-tossed Bay, and nosed into the winding creek. Plumpy followed a short distance behind.

As he trailed the *Bay-Rovers*, caution suddenly rippled through him; but it was more the warning memory of these alligator-infested bayous than fear of the new motor boat. The *Bay-Rovers* intrigued him more than ever. Plumpy's curiosity about odd-looking things was almost as keen as the curiosity of the raccoons that dwelt on these jungle islands.

He followed the boat for several hundred winding yards. The channel was too narrow here for him to blow out his breath alongside. Storm howled overhead, clawing at the overhanging trees, but the creek water was almost smooth.

When they reached a deep cove, Plumpy at once skirled ahead through the tidewater. His upward roll and *whoof* of breath were lusty, for he meant to be heard by the boatmen.

A tousled head bearing a slouchy felt hat bent over the port side of the launch. "Talkin' about them sea-hogs," exclaimed the man, "here's one of 'em now!"

Another bearded face peered through the creek's gloom. "Say! I betcha that's the little porpoise we tried to net up with his mother!"

The pilot spoke a word of warning. "Don't bother him. Act friendly. A porpoise has got sense: He can tell a friendly boat from other kinds. Let him follow us on in. We'll get a skiff and net this time—one that he cain't bust apart!"

The other fishermen chuckled their approval. "Good! That buyer we was talkin' to about porpoise blubber said he'd like to have a sample, so's he can tell us how much it's worth."

Feeling sure that this was a friendly boat, Plumpy continued to follow as it wound on up the creek. He was looking for storm shelter anyway. The *Bay-Rovers* finally pushed her prow into a large hidden bayou. At the back crook of this cove, the jungle had been cleared away. Several ugly cabins stood a few steps from the tidewater. This was the hiding place of the Pirate Island seine-crew!

But Plumpy didn't know that.

The launch was tied up at a crude little pier. The men got out. "Better make it snappy," said one of them. "Get a net-skiff, an' shove back to the neck of the creek. This porpoise is a frisky young bull. Probably won't hurry out. We'll strip him to blubber, sure!"

Plumpy rolled about in the bayou, exploring all its curves and deeper nooks. He snapped up a stray silver mullet. Strange smells came to his nostrils when he rose to refill his lungs. They were the odors of stale fish, and the scent of man-foods.

Plumpy began to feel uneasy.

A skiff was moving cautiously toward the neck of the nearby creek, a stout new net stacked in its stern.

Plumpy slid to the middle of the cove. He lay still for a moment, trying to sense just what sort of place this was. Man-sounds vibrated the water. A light shove of the skiff came to his ears. The man-sounds became rumbling, gloating laughter!

Plumpy, sensing danger, slid toward the creek. But already the net-skiff had reached it! Quickly the boatman had stretched the strong net across the stream. A heavy lead-line held the bottom against the creek-floor; the cork-line floated at the top. Between the two lines, the broad net sagged in dangerous folds.

Not satisfied with that, the man tied another length to a tree, and stretched it two feet high across the stream. He then swung his skiff lengthwise against the net, and with a shout of triumph, signaled that he was ready. "All set! Now drive that little sea-pig this way!"

Plumpy, sure now that something was wrong, circled around in perplexity. Another skiff had left the net-racks near the camp. It was lining out another net around the suspicious porpoise.

Plumpy darted back toward the creek. But he sensed the waiting net a dozen yards away. Somersaulting he sped across the bayou. The other net had already circled him.

Plumpy swirled violently in the water. A trap! That's what his curiosity had led him into!

More of the Pirate Island men had poled out to watch the cruel fun. The seine, which was stretched completely around Plumpy, was being drawn in, and he was being forced gradually forward toward the blocked creek! He dared not touch the net, lest he become entangled. But the other seine was being drawn closer and closer to him.

Plumpy was desperate. He somersaulted angrily, *whoofed* threateningly. But the evil men only laughed. One of them stood upright in the blocking skiff, holding a short staff in his hands. At one end was a coiled rope. At the other end was a three-pronged harpoon!

The water now boiled about Plumpy's agitated body. He was confined in a space less than twenty yards across—and it was being drawn smaller all the time!

The man who held the dangerous harpoon stood ready, weapon poised.

Plumpy suddenly grew still. His rounded head came above water once more. His crafty little eyes regarded the nets and the skiff that blocked his escape. Then he disappeared.

Next moment, beginning at the farthest possible point, he set his torpedo-like form into motion so swift that the fishermen could scarcely see him. He charged straight for the blockading skiff-net!

"Now we'll get him!" yelled the waiting men.

"I'll harpoon him, soon's he gets——"

The fisherman never finished his threat. Within a few feet of the creek-net there was a terrific explosion of water. The next instant Plumpy was in the air—gliding upward like a solid dark rocket![1]

Cries of amazement came from the men. They crouched in their boats. The harpoon man lost his balance, and fell backward into the water. There was a flashing glimpse of a white belly, as the young porpoise cleared the boat. A loud splash on the other side told that Plumpy had landed in free water!

Behind him, the water foamed, and waves rocked the light skiffs up and down. Furious words could now be heard. But Plumpy the porpoise lost no time in that tidewater creek. He was scooting along as never before, headed for the open Bay.

[1] The author has known porpoises to leap over fishing skiffs.

PLUMPY VENTURES INTO THE BIG DEEP

THE squall had passed over by the time Plumpy emerged into
the Bay, and the late afternoon sun was shining again. Only
a faint choppiness disturbed the surface. Plumpy halted, and
drank in great lungfuls of storm-freshened air. He felt excited,
but no longer fearful. Hadn't he come out of that tight place
victorious?

He let the mixed vibrations of his watery world play through
his body. Strongest of those signals was the mysterious song of
the open Gulf. It seemed to be calling him into other adven-

tures—adventures more exciting and wonderful than any he'd known!

He turned his snout up Pirate Bay.

The deep water of Hurricane Pass showed more green than blue today. Dimly he remembered his early experience here, the time the great shark had almost got him. But that seemed a long time ago. Plumpy was now twice as large, and twice as old. Besides, the young porpoise had proved himself competent in several dangerous escapades. Even old Black-Porp was coming to recognize his powers.

The lure of the great green Gulf whispered outside the Pass. Plumpy swam through. He encountered no sharks. The recent squall had chased them, too, into more secluded hideaways.

Out of the Pass, the adventuring porpoise idled a moment. Above him lay a glittering white beach made brilliant with a million shells of every color. Before him, endlessly, spread the great mysterious Gulf!

Without further ado, Plumpy turned his black back upon Pirate Bay, and headed bravely into the unknown deep.

He had no definite thoughts of his herd just then. Perhaps instinct gave him that strange urge to go a-conquering. The sea grew deeper, less green, more blue. Varied creatures began to appear; golden pompano, red snappers, bluefish. Once a huge jewfish, yellow-mottled and ugly, rose sullenly from the depths. Quickly, at sight of Plumpy's own forbidding bulk and fearless manner, it sank again.

The wandering porpoise soon burst into an enormous school

of mullet which the recent squall had driven from the Bay. For once, Plumpy was not hungry and made no attempt to seize any of the fish. His senses were completely centered on adventure. But the mullet fled in terror, skipping along the surface in frantic haste. This ready respect gave Plumpy even more self-assurance, and he plowed on, straight out to sea.

The porpoise usually confines its excursions to surface depths. A conqueror, though, should explore all quarters, so Plumpy filled his lungs with a supply of air, and sank a few fathoms. He saw creatures of freakish and ferocious appearance, but small in size. Whenever they appeared unwilling to give way, he arrogantly nosed into them.

He saw queer-shaped rayfish with blots for bodies and shoe-strings for tails. A huge sea turtle, with corrugated, impenetrable shell and leathery green flippers, swam over him.

Alert with soaring curiosity, Plumpy slid toward this lumbering creature. He whipped his powerful tail sharply upward. The sea churned soundlessly under the weight of the deep water. The impact jolted the great turtle slightly off balance, and it slithered away in a ridiculous sidewise course. The jarring blow also tilted Plumpy head downward. Surprised, he quickly leveled out and away from that neighborhood. His tail quivered from the bruise inflicted by contact with that horny shell.

As he nosed toward the surface, another bulky thing hove into view, a creature as horrible in looks as it was mammoth in size. As broad across as a boat, this flat monster rippled toward the horrified porpoise. Its mouth was an enormous, yawning disc of bone that looked capable of swallowing everything in sight.

Plumpy's one brief glimpse was enough. He fled like a streak of lightning, leaving a swirling wake as straight as a bullet's course.

Plumpy did not know it, but despite the devilfish's two tons of bulk and shockingly ugly head, it really feeds on minnows and other tiny sea-life.

It was now that the wandering porpoise experienced his first touch of homesickness. Perhaps, after all, this exploring and conquering business was silly! In his memory appeared the blue, peaceful waters of his home Bay. They seemed already very far behind him. For a moment he toyed with the desire to return to his family. Just then, however, a blue shadow crossed his line of vision. Mackerel! Plumpy suddenly felt empty, and with a hungry rush he went after the fleeing fish. His appetite was soon satisfied.

Every creature of the deep was taking notice of him, knew he was rapidly becoming king of the vast gulf! He cruised on blithely into the setting sun.

By the time he had covered another league, the sun had set and the light had disappeared from the sky. Now the Gulf seemed to grow vaster and vaster. Greenish fire flashed and wavered. The lone porpoise saw a thousand different trails, as a thousand different creatures moved about him in the black water. Some of them were small streaks of weird fire. Others were large and restless, the wakes of creatures strange to the Bay porpoise.

Plumpy's loneliness deepened. Homesickness for Pirate Bay

and for his own herd throbbed within him. What wonderful times he had enjoyed in those pleasant blue reaches of water! How playful and friendly were his own family, and how strange and hostile everything seemed out here in the immense open Gulf!

He was afraid to go to sleep. Some huge monster might find him and devour him in one hungry gulp! He kept moving, aimlessly, very unsure of himself. What would happen to him out here? Maybe even the warm red sun would fail to come up! Plumpy trembled with fear.

A FLASHING SWORD—AND A HURRICANE

THE great red sun did come up at last. It seemed to bound up out of the sea itself, spreading down a hot warmth upon a becalmed water. The Gulf was so still and smooth this morning, it looked almost as if oil might have been poured over its sea-green surface.

Plumpy climbed eagerly to the air, probably the earliest one of the larger fishes to disturb that vast expanse. He was so happy to see the cheerful sunlight that he lolled for a long time about the surface.

Then he rolled off in search of his breakfast.

He came into a small school of Gulf-snappers. But, delicious as he sensed them to be, they were much too large for his jaws. Some of them were as long as his own body!

Plumpy moved on.

A long finny sail sliced the water, coming in his direction. Plumpy halted, instantly on guard. What strange creature was this?

He saw it, then. It was a shiny, blue-colored fish twice as long as a porpoise! A foot-long spike, dagger-keen, stuck out from its nose!

Plumpy snorted in helpless fright, and quickly submarined downward.

The great blue sailfish leaped lightly into the sunlight, its tapering body glinting like clean blue steel. It struck water with a thunderous splash, and streaked on about its own business of finding breakfast. The sailfish had no interest in porpoise meat!

Plumpy trailed for another hungry hour. Still he found no food. There did not seem to be many creatures in the Gulf by day, and those that he did meet were large fishes.

Plumpy tried a new course. Presently he came to a stop. Water trembled ahead. Food-fish?

The porpoise strained his senses to identify them. Mullet, dead ahead!

He rolled forward noiselessly and came into the thick school with crafty determination. He was so hungry he didn't wait to play flip-in-the-air with them. He simply shoved in among them with mouth agape. Before the school had spread and vanished, the porpoise had crunched a number of mullet, and slid the delicious hash into his stomach.

The tide turned with unusual pressure. Plumpy could tell the difference as he propelled his sleek form through it. He was still roving farther into the Gulf, although the uneasiness he had felt the night before had not entirely left him. But with his stomach again satisfied, the porpoise felt more encouraged.

The open Gulf remained devoid of wind. On his frequent visits to the surface, Plumpy felt the sun's sultry heat pressing down upon the water. A warmer smell of salt tide, a heavier blend of fishy odors, played in his nostrils.

When next he came up for air, he sighted, far in the distance, a sailing vessel. It didn't seem to be moving at all.

Aquiver with eagerness for some friendly sight, Plumpy headed straight for the ship.

It was a large craft, a Cuban snapper boat. The sails were slack and lifeless. She was becalmed at sea.

The porpoise warily circled the great vessel twice, keeping himself invisible and unheard. Man-sounds filtered through the water to him. They didn't sound hostile. The ship herself seemed friendly.

Plumpy boiled up alongside, *whoofing* loudly. Nothing happened. He dived and rolled up once more, but the dark-skinned sailors aboard paid little attention to the frisking porpoise. The reason for this was that the crew was worried. They wanted to

make land with all possible speed.

"Thees too-hot calm, I theenk she mean a hurricane come," remarked the swarthy captain of the fishing smack.

"*Si*. Yes," agreed the mate. "And the storm she come before many hours, I theenk."

The brown faces of all the sailors were marked with concern. If they got no breeze, the hurricane would hit them far from land, and demolish them.

Understanding none of this talk, Plumpy tried again to attract their attention, but he was unsuccessful.

"The wind blow!" cried a sailor.

Sails began to flutter with returning hope. A faint breeze, hot and electric, rippled the water's surface. Sailors began to move briskly aboard the fishing smack.

The porpoise, still rolling alongside, felt the vessel stir. Sails were swelling in the rising wind, and the ship gathered speed.

Plumpy followed for a short distance, but the boat moved too slowly to interest him. He dropped away from the stern, and cruised off in a different course.

As the wind increased, Plumpy sensed a new vibration in the water. A warning was being broadcast throughout the vast liquid underworld. It was not the warning of dangerous monsters, but a wavering, rising signal of more widespread danger.

To the porpoise it was vaguely like the mysterious song of the Gulf he used to hear while roving at night in his home waters. But now it crooned with a steadily increasing whine.

Suddenly Plumpy was moving through the water. His instincts recognized that wavering signal. It meant that far out at sea leagues and fathoms of brine were raging under the fury of a great storm!

Even to the creatures of the sea, whose home is the water, the voice of a hurricane is a voice of disaster.

Plumpy decided to go home.

But many turns of the tide lay between him and Pirate Bay. It would prove a long trip back, with constant high speed to keep ahead of the storm. There would be no time for fishing or for rest. It would mean steady, tireless going.

Plumpy's instincts were truer than a ship's compass. He set off unerringly in the direction of Hurricane Pass. To avoid the now rolling surface of the Gulf, he kept to an even four-foot depth. The water was not yet rough down there.

Something sizzled across Plumpy's tail with startling unexpectedness. His body instantly grew tense with alarm. What he saw was only a blur, but a moment later the hostile fish had circled.

It was a giant swordfish! Its six-foot body was armed with a bony, rapier-like blade that was itself as long as Plumpy's entire body. Agitated by the approaching hurricane, and always in a mean humor, the monster seemed eager to thrust that keen blade through anything it met.

Again the scaleless, finny body tilted toward the porpoise. With a convulsive wriggle, Plumpy eluded the thrust. Instinct warned him that here, at last, was a deadly foe!

The swordfish is a true pirate of the sea. Powerful, vicious, stubbornly persistent, its sword is always unsheathed for instant use.

It made a furious quick loop in the water, then again sped toward the porpoise. One wicked thrust, and Plumpy's sleek body would be mortally punctured!

The sea was growing rougher. The turbulent voice of the Gulf was telegraphing its signals of the roaring hurricane. But Plumpy was too busy to heed the warning. Right here was a menace more deadly than a hurricane!

HURRICANE FURY

IT seemed that the fighting swordfish was possessed with the fury of the oncoming storm itself. Could there be any reason why he should wish to kill a friendly porpoise? Possibly the sworded monster aspired to be Emperor of the Gulf!

The blade of the great fish circled again, like a cutlass swung by a pirate's hand. Leveling out, it tilted in a hissing streak for Plumpy's side. The horrified porpoise beheld the monster's big round eyes, that looked like glass door-knobs with an evil color in their centers.

The swordfish is swift, but the porpoise, too, is famous for quickness of movement. Plumpy set his muscles. Downward he shot in one swift streak. The keen blade of the fish knifed passed him, not an inch from his sleek skin.

Already Plumpy could hear the rippling hiss of that blade circling again. Like a submarine with all engines geared to full speed ahead, the porpoise made every fiber in his powerful young body do double duty. He sped away, traveling twice as fast as the fleetest naval submarine!

Behind him, the enraged swordfish whirled about in futile circles. It had lost Plumpy's trail. Still in an evil humor, it finally pointed its blade in a different direction, and streaked away. It, too, had to seek refuge from the hurricane now sweeping toward them.

Never relaxing his swift pace, never forgetting the vibrations of the storm, Plumpy churned on his homeward course. Though no land was in sight, he knew that Hurricane Pass lay dead ahead.

Ten leagues Plumpy navigated before he slackened his speed. Then powerful as he was, he began to tire. He cut down to an even cruising pace, then kept valiantly on his set course.

Before he could reach Hurricane Pass, the storm struck. He could feel the billowing fury of the surface waters, when he went up for air. He was rolled and tumbled by the roaring waves. The skies were black.

Plumpy submerged quickly, and plowed on through the turbulent sea, fighting every foot of the way. A powerful undertow, like the mingling of several powerful streams, clutched at his speeding form. He must reach the Pass!

Again the porpoise had to rise for fresh air. Again the tremendous waves tossed him mercilessly. His usual *whoof* of breath was now jerked from him in long wheezing grunts. Battered and tiring rapidly, the lone voyager ruddered to the depths once more. How far he had come! How his muscles ached with weariness! Would he ever reach Hurricane Pass, and the refuge of his beloved Bay?

Much later, as Plumpy once more fought the turbulent surface, he sensed that land lay hard ahead. The night was as black as ink. But Plumpy knew beyond a doubt he had arrived at Hurricane Pass!

Happy as this made him, he knew that he now faced another battle. He was like a submarine fighting out of a raging sea, trying to make safe harbor. The storm waves swept him violently toward shore. If he were washed upon the land he would be done for.

Plumpy was all but exhausted. He strained every ounce of his remaining strength to guide himself carefully into the narrow Pass. His weary brain suddenly warned him that the next surge of water could either hurl him into the channel of the dark Pass or would pound him senseless against rocky ground.

With a powerful wriggle of his body, Plumpy braced himself and squared his nose for the deeper channel. Would he pass through?

The next instant, as the sea pitched him like a chip, the porpoise felt sandy surface brush hard against his thick hide. He gave a desperate wriggle to port as the sand-wall slid past him. Like a streamlined rocket, Plumpy hurtled through Hurricane Pass.

His beloved home waters were now tossing violently under the sweeping storm. Plumpy knew that he would have to find a cove protected from the wind, in quiet water, before he could pause for rest.

Vaguely, his instincts had already revealed to him where his refuge lay. It was a snug bayou, deep among the thick mangrove jungle of Seagrape Island. There the water would be less rough, and there he could idle while the furious winds passed over.

Plumpy was driven half across the Bay, however, before he arrived opposite the cove he sought. Now he ruddered about, half-heading into the teeth of the storm. Wearily he fought forward. Every roll gained meant a terrific strain on his remaining strength. He let his senses take new soundings.

After another half-hour of battling the seething Bay, Plumpy rocked into the tidewater creek. It was much deeper than usual. He pressed his nose ahead. Already he felt relieved.

At long last, exhausted, battered, and sore in every muscle of his body, the lone porpoise reached his snug haven. He blew out his pent-up breath in a prolonged sigh of relief. Then, refilling his lungs, he quickly slid down into the deepest pot-hole he could find.

Out in the Bay, and far out in the great Gulf, mountainous waves continued to crash one upon another. Plumpy, numbed with weariness, could still hear the great sea's siren song of mystery. It droned and howled and wavered, on and on and on.

But for Plumpy, that mysterious song had now no luring voice. He had been to sea and he didn't like it. He was glad to be home again, snug in a safe retreat. He sank into deep sleep.

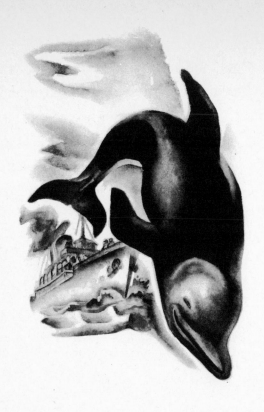

PLUMPY RESCUES A STEAMBOAT

THROUGHOUT the night the storm roared. Finally a driving deluge of rain was added to the mighty lashing of wind. It offered an eerie accompaniment to the howling symphony of the Gulf. Plumpy still rested. His body, close to the miry sea-floor, swayed gently. At regular intervals he slid up for air.

When daylight broke, Plumpy aroused himself from slumber. His body felt stiff, and his stomach empty and flat. But here was another day. He felt a sudden longing for his beloved herd.

Had they passed safely through the storm? And where would they be?

The Bay waters still rocked restlessly, but the hurricane was slackening in fury. It was safe now for a porpoise to move about at will. Besides, Plumpy was hungrier than he'd ever been in his life. He must find food to restore his energy.

Noon came, still sunless but brighter. Plumpy had found no food, but time and again, a tantalizing variety of food-smells came to him. Mullet, trout, mackerel, bluefish—and countless odors which were new to the young porpoise. But the storm had so mixed them together that Plumpy could not trace their present location. His hungry stomach gnawed beseechingly, Food! Food!

He crisscrossed the Bay, and roved up Gulf Sound, but found only a lot of wreckage swirling about. He again traversed the length of Pirate Bay.

Suddenly, as the porpoise rose to the surface, he sighted the *Palm Scout*. Black smoke billowed thickly from her stack. She rolled and pitched in the wake of the storm as she headed out from Seagrape Island. She appeared uncertain of her direction.

For once in his thirty years of command, Captain McKinley was not sure of his course. True, Pirate Bay was only four miles across. Land was always in sight. But the *Palm Scout* had to follow a narrow channel, and today the seasoned Captain could see no markers!

He jingled the pilot's signal. Below, the engineer cut the engine's speed. The steamer pitched in the lessening seas.

"The hurricane has swept away the buoy-markers," called the captain. His voice held concern. Here the channel turned constantly, and if the *Palm Scout* missed it just once, she would be grounded. There was still enough force in the waves to pound her old hulk to wreckage.

Captain McKinley, hidden in the pilot's cabin, trod sharply on the bell. That was the signal to stop the engines. His voice then boomed out: "Cast anchor! We'll drift aground quickly. Water's so muddy I can't see where the channel begins or where it ends!"

The anchor dropped with a leaden splash.

"That'll hold us for a few minutes," said Captain McKinley, "but we still can't find our way."

At this point, another figure came on deck, and paused on braced legs opposite the pilot's cabin. It was young Warden Gregg. He was focusing his alert eyes on the nearby water. He had just noticed a disturbance there.

Next moment, out of the rolling waves came a blunt round head, and Plumpy the porpoise blew out his breath in greeting.

"Here!" cried Warden Gregg to the captain. "I think we can move ahead now, sir. Here's one of our Bay pilots."

The gray-haired captain hurried to the rail, and glanced down. Plumpy was somersaulting friskily, despite his sore muscles and unfed stomach.

"Yes," decided the captain with relief. "The porpoise will keep us in the channel. We'll put in at the next pier until the water clears. I can tell how the channel runs, when the water is calm; right now it's a stroke of luck having a guide!''

Plumpy understood nothing about the steamer's plight, but he did know, from long experience, that the *Palm Scout* always followed the channel. So he had learned to lead the way. Sailors weighed anchor. The steamboat churned slightly. Immediately the porpoise rolled ahead. His shining dark form marked a course that was easy to follow. If he dived, he came up immediately, still safely within the channel.

On deck, Warden Gregg chuckled. "I've heard of porpoises guiding ships, but this is the first time I've ever been rescued by one myself."

"Intelligent creatures," said the captain earnestly. "I know my way now. There lies Buttonwood pier; though I see the hurricane has pretty badly stripped it."

When the *Palm Scout* blasted her whistle, and put in carefully for the storm-damaged pier, Plumpy fell away. He rocked off through the water, the rolling sea giving his motion a distinct swagger. Perhaps even the porpoise, in his animal brain, realized that he had rescued his old friends, the *Palm Scout* and her genial captain.

Though Plumpy roved through more miles of fish-hunting, he found nothing fit to eat. Here and there he encountered storm-killed fishes. But a porpoise is particular about his food. He prefers to kill and consume it while it is fresh. Plumpy would have none of this shark's garbage. Mid-afternoon came, and all he had found to eat was a twelve-inch needlefish and one flat sunfish, circling fretfully about a submerged stake. That scant meal didn't begin to satisfy his ravenous hunger.

It was as he turned aimlessly into East Sound that an idea, and the grim determination to carry it out, came to him. The old sunken pirate ship! Perhaps he could find more of those deliciously sweet octopuses there. He was so hungry that he felt almost up to tackling the horrid old demon of the slimy cabin.

Plumpy nosed resolutely up the Sound his round mouth beginning to water with anticipation. So dazzling was this vision of food, that he ignored the sudden prickles of warning which rippled through his body.

PLUMPY IS CARRIED TO HOSPITAL BAYOU

THE rain and wind abated, but a drab gloom still pressed down over the Bay. Black-Porp had been anxiously hunting up and down the empty waters, seeking food for his weakened herd. Though the old leader and his family had retreated to deep hidden pot-holes when the storm first rose, every member was now tired, and thin with hunger. Black-Porp had missed Plumpy, the strayed yearling. Where had he been during the fierce hurricane? What had happened to him?

The old herd-bull didn't know the answers to all these instinctive questions; he felt only a growing anxiety about Plumpy's safety. Just now, though, the seasoned leader was more concerned with finding food for his herd.

Cutting a diagonal course down the churned waters of Pirate Bay, Black-Porp finally rolled into the vicinity of East Sound. He paused there, his herdlings at his flanks in the chill water. He detected no presence of food-fish, but to his weary senses came a double signal.

What was wrong here? Black-Porp looked solemn and worried as he idled in the Sound, letting the storm-mixed vibrations play through his great body. Faintly he detected the distant, smooth-rolling movements of a member of his herd. Could it be Plumpy the wanderer? There was no other solitary porpoise in Pirate Bay.

The old herd-bull felt certain it was Plumpy. What disturbed him more was the other part of that underwater signal. Even more faintly it came, almost imperceptible even to an experienced leader.

Anxious about his herd, and filled with growing suspicion about the future safety of Pirate Bay, Black-Porp felt both relief and grave apprehension. Plumpy, the wilful but beloved member of his friendly herd, was alive! The hurricane hadn't battered him to death, after all. But wait—what was the meaning of this other slight commotion? Was Plumpy in some new trouble?

Instantly the loyal old herd-bull forgot his own hunger. He charged swiftly up the Sound, the herd following in wonder.

Black-Porp had suddenly remembered the old sunken wreckage. More alarming, he remembered that he had long suspected the presence of some merciless and fiendish thing which inhabited that slimy old hull.

The hungry porpoise herd rolled swiftly up East Sound. If the strayed Plumpy was again in trouble, his family must help him.

Plumpy himself had reached the point where the old sunken galleon lay. His mind was so occupied with the thought of food that he was not aware of the near presence of the herd. He refilled his lungs with a full store of oxygen. He dived, lean, desperately hungry, determined to feed.

The slimy green hulk of wreckage had not been moved by the furious hurricane. Indeed, many, many tropical storms had howled over Pirate Bay since human pirates were cleared from this evil sloop and it had been sunk to become the brig of water-demons. But last night's hurricane had jostled and beat against the wreckage; a few more of its rotting timbers had caved in.

Plumpy circled it once. He saw nothing. No sea-life moved here. No baby octopuses scuttled before his hungry, questing nose. Had the storm swept the old hull barren?

Plumpy's stomach began to ache with disappointment. Wasn't he to eat, even here? His last chance—and no food.

Deliberately the porpoise slid toward the yawning cabin. A timber sagged above its door. The water all around was a sickly green. The porpoise halted at the threshold, and peered inside. Nothing moved. Not the least tremble seemed to justify the prickle of warning which again pulsed through the porpoise's senses.

Plumpy pushed his bulk through the gaping doorway. Suspended in the liquid-green cavity of the ancient pilot-room, he peered hopefully about him. Across the cabin a brighter green marked an old window. Plumpy swung about slowly. There were slime-covered seats, and the pilot's arm-rest, also thick with green scum. The porpoise turned farther in his careful inspection. There loomed a round something, with spokes and knobbed ends—the pilot's-wheel.

But nothing moved. Below him, beneath the round wheel, the gloom was deeper. Dark with a ghostly darkness, its quiet mystery could not be penetrated by Plumpy's watchful eyes. There the cabin floor had rotted through, leaving an enormous cavity in the hold.

Plumpy swung slowly, reluctantly, around. Food! food! cried his suffering insides. But there was no food.

The porpoise went suddenly rigid. The gloomy water was throbbing faintly. *Something* was moving!

Before Plumpy could turn his nose about for a good look, the mysterious presence of the ghostly old pirate ship was upon him—a yellowish globe, blue-mottled, horrible! In his brief glimpse of it, the porpoise realized with swift apprehension that the thing had grown even huger since his first frightened visit!

What happened then was too quick for thought. Long elastic arms suddenly clamped around Plumpy. They contracted with a deadly power. Plumpy felt his gaunt form fairly caving in.

A grunt was pressed from him. Bubbles spiralled upward from his opening nostrils. He was locked in the death-grip of the old octopus—the demon of the sunken galleon!

Plumpy had known fear many times before. Never until now had he known such horror. He was being squeezed in the clutch of eight powerful arms—arms which had changed from rubbery suppleness to bands of steel!

The porpoise tried desperately to wriggle. He seemed unable to move. With a strength born of terror, he flapped his protruding tail. Water swirled. He flapped even more frantically. The cabin became a boiling cauldron. The gripped and the evil gripper whirled as one body about the cabin. Plumpy smashed against a slimy wall and rebounded crazily toward another. Desperately he tried to move his trapped body toward the yawning doorway. Always the eight-armed monster, eyes bulging, yanked him away.

Plumpy's vision became a whirling reel of blurred doorways and windows, all made horrible by the murky green of the churning water. Compressed sounds throbbed throughout the waterlogged ship.

More and more desperately the porpoise heaved his frantic tail. The pair whirled over and over, and Plumpy's empty stomach felt pressed as flat as a flounder! His brain throbbed dizzily.

With an abrupt buckle of his cramped body and a last mighty lash of his tail, the porpoise hurled both himself and the octopus against a wall. Water-rotted timbers gave way. The grimly fighting bodies burst into open water!

This unexpected action jarred loose the demon's hold. An ugly, suction-cupped tentacle dangled before Plumpy's eyes. Instantly he clamped his jaws about it and cut through with his teeth.

The octopus was convulsed with fury. Plumpy bolted ahead, but before he was quite free of those clutching tentacles, he saw the globular body move its limber arms like an umbrella being rapidly opened and closed. At the same moment a foul, inky darkness stained the waters. The octopus had discharged its fountain of sepia—that telltale challenge of a fight to the death!

Momentarily blinded by this nauseous discoloration, Plumpy wavered uncertainly. A second later he was again seized by the demon-fish and clutched in a firmer grip than before. He felt his lungs almost bursting. Still he struggled with desperate courage. The porpoise's own nature was as grim and stubborn as the octopus, once his fighting spirit had been aroused. He fought for the surface. The octopus fought with equal grimness for the darker depths.

Plumpy was fast being exhausted. He had battled leagues of hurricane-swept tide. It had been many hours since he had consumed enough food. But more horrifying now than the fear of exhaustion was the deadly pressure of those sucking tentacles.

Moment by moment the porpoise felt them biting into his hide, deeper and deeper. Each of those deadly bands seemed to possess a rough-edged knife. As tough and thick as the porpoise knew his leathery hide to be, he knew also that it was being torn!

The body of the octopus, like a pot solid with evil hatred, was clamped so tightly against the porpoise's back that the monster's horrid eyes seemed bulging from their sockets! From within that mottled globe the sea-demon's final and most hideous work was about to be done.

Plumpy was convulsed with pain and terror as he felt two metal-hard points begin to bore into his back. The cuttlebone beak of the octopus, hidden in its leathery mantle, was rapidly seeking an opening into the porpoise's vital flesh!

Such fury as Plumpy had never felt before suddenly possessed him. With the frenzied action born of valiant will-power, he fought with every atom, forcing his numbed senses into one last mad effort. He heaved. He writhed. He tried to leap with his deadly burden. His body swelled with blind rage.

As this terrific exertion taxed his energies to the breaking-point, he flattened his body. He felt the sucking, scraping tentacles slip their hold. He bolted forward, slipped free of the monster's clutch!

That did not end Plumpy's fury. He whirled, water boiling. Sickening sepia again darkened the water—and he got only a vague glimpse of the octopus darting toward him like an evil cloud.

Plumpy didn't hesitate. He charged blindly and got inside the reaching arms of his enemy. He felt the globular body strike his snout like a mass of rubber. The porpoise's jaws flew open, and clamped shut on a vital part.

The huge mouthful he crunched from the devilfish slid into Plumpy's battered stomach, as he snatched a second one from the mottled form. The tentacles writhed madly, desperately, but the strength had gone out of them. The octopus quivered slightly, and began to settle in the water. Then it slowly turned over and sank to the bottom of the Sound.

Plumpy was too numb with exhaustion, too groggy in his brain, to follow the evil thing. His lungs were bursting for want of fresh air. Hardly able to wriggle, he crawled upward. It seemed to take him a long, long time to reach the surface. He scarcely knew when he got there. A leaden feeling settled over him. Had the horrible devilfish slain him, after all?

Plumpy had a vague, weird sensation of floating for long hours on the choppy surface of the Bay. Finally he had the blurred sense of something shoving him, moving his battered body along through the water. But he was too tired to protest. If other enemies were now after him, he had no strength left to defend himself.

But no new enemy was attacking Plumpy. Black-Porp had found him. The herd-bull had sensed Plumpy's violent struggle a mile away. Ever loyal to any member of his herd, the leader had hurried along with his family.

Though old Black-Porp was distressed to find the yearling Plumpy so battered and seemingly lifeless, he felt a stir of pride in his great body. He knew that Plumpy had conquered the fiendish devilfish; for the seasoned old porpoise leader knew from personal experience that whenever a full-grown octopus engages in battle it is a fight to the finish.

Black-Porp's herd gently propelled Plumpy's still form out of the Sound. Far up a winding creek, the old leader found a body of still water. This was "Hospital Bayou," so named because here crippled creatures of the sea retreated to recover from various injuries. No preying sharks entered this quiet cove. No scavenger fishes found their way into it. Here in the peaceful shadows of the surrounding mangroves Plumpy was left. If he was not too far gone, the healing ways of Nature would restore him to health.

Then old Black-Porp turned his still-hungry herd back down the winding creek. A difficult task lay before them. They must find food. If they didn't, they themselves might become patients in Hospital Bayou!

MULLET-ROE SEASON

TROPIC sunshine again blessed land and water. Pirate Bay regained its sparkle of tranquil blue. Fishing boats once more limped up and down the Bay.

A score of tides turned in and out of Hospital Bayou before Plumpy stirred into actual wakefulness. He found himself suspended in a warm pot-hole. Overhanging trees circled the hidden cove. On all sides of Plumpy's sandy berth lay shallows, glinting a warm yellow under the sunshine which struck through the tree tops.

The hole in which the porpoise had been left to recover was sufficiently deep for him to submerge when necessary. Against its sloping banks his battle-scarred body could loll and bask in the healing sunshine.

The porpoise was still sore in every part of his frame. He didn't feel like moving. His stomach was empty, but he had no appetite. Awake, he continued to bask in the sun, feeling only a torpid indifference.

At night the moon changed from a round golden disc to a silver sickle. Then one day, when the high sun struck shallows and pot-holes with equal warmth, Plumpy felt the pulsing of re-newed life. Pleasant smells again came to him. He began to heed the telegraphic vibrations which reached him through the water. Somewhere out there, beyond this winding arm of land, fish were moving. Food-fish!

Almost instantly Plumpy felt hungry. He wriggled his body experimentally. His muscles jumped and quivered, but the soreness had vanished. Beyond the golden shallows a sand-perch flipped lightly. The porpoise felt a quick desire to do some tail-flipping himself.

He circled his limited berth. The tide was low. Shallow water surrounded him. He could not leave his hospital berth just yet but the more he moved, the stronger he felt and the keener grew his appetite. His stomach was just a foodless cavity.

At flood-tide, Plumpy was able to leave his invalid's berth. He nosed eagerly out of the creek. How good it was to see the open Bay once more! How delightful the water felt! What an appetizing blend of fish-odors teased his nostrils!

He picked up speed as he swam. A mullet leaped just ahead. Plumpy darted for it, knocked it into the air, and caught it, though the action reminded him that his scars were still sensitive. That gulp of food, however, caused his appetite to beg for more. What a long, long time it had been since his stomach had been filled and happy!

A plan began forming in his sharpening senses. He pushed his gaunt, worn frame on up the Bay, and turned north. The sheer cliffs of Shell-Bank Key shone ahead.

Plumpy halted there, neither heeding nor caring about the long sawfish blade which still lay there bleaching in the sun. He promptly hid himself behind the sharp turn of the shell-cliff. The tide would be running out, and fish would be passing.

The trick worked. A school of mullet, all unsuspecting, filed past the cliff. Plumpy charged into them with ravenous hunger, and devoured enough fat bodies to feel comfortably full for the first time in days.

That same afternoon he encountered proof that he would not be long regaining his former sleekness. In the upper reach of Pirate Bay he came upon a vast school of mullet. The water was black with them. Gulls and other sea-birds were hovering overhead, shrilling with wild elation. Plumpy cut a gluttonous course through the heart of the milling school. They tasted better than ever. Fatter, sweeter, richer! Plumpy ate until he was stuffed with the nourishing fare.

Roe season had come. Each mullet and trout was round with

egg-roe. This season of abundance would last for weeks. Hour by hour Plumpy could feel his emaciated frame taking on flesh and strength.

It was another fortnight before he found his herd. Plumpy was overjoyed at sight of his family. He frisked into their midst feeling no damage from that horrible battle with the octopus.

Old Black-Porp and the other herdlings saw the difference in him. Plumpy was fatter than he'd ever been, and he had grown a good six inches longer; but slantwise across his side lay a dull gray streak, almost livid against his darker body. There the demon of the pirate ship had scored a lasting mark! But Plumpy wasn't conscious of this scar. He felt so lusty and so filled with reborn strength that he was certain he had never looked so fine.

Old Black-Porp's action confirmed that conceit. The old herd-bull, whose own aging body was marked with a dozen lasting scars, evidently considered Plumpy's mark a badge of honor—the memento of a terrific battle courageously won.

For another dozen tides, the porpoise herd fed together, waxing even fatter. The roe season would soon be over, and the porpoises, aware of the fact, seemed bent on storing up all the blubber and energy they could. Food-fish would not be so abundant during the winter months close at hand.

For this reason, the porpoises lost some of their caution. Even old Black-Porp, stuffing himself till he seemed about to burst, forgot to be grouchy and relaxed his vigilance.

Until the past few weeks, fishing boats had been a common

sight in the Bay. Then, following the storm, fish had been scarce. When they began to run again, every fisherman worked double time. But with the beginning of roe season, this activity halted. Roe season was closed to fishermen by law.

Unfortunately for the porpoises, however, the seine crew from Pirate Island was more active than ever. With their new, faster launch they trailed a dozen skiffs furtively up and down the Bay. Sometimes, too, the porpoises heard the whine of a speed-boat streaking through the Bay.

The unlawful gang of seiners took heavy toll of the spawning mullet. They salted away the fat roe, to be peddled later, unknown to young Warden Gregg. When the season ended, even the Pirate Islanders no longer had anything to keep them busy.

"Now about them porpoises," remarked a member of that crew one evening. They were sprawled lazily around their campfire, planning schemes to make more money. "I think," the man contined, "that them sea-hogs are fat aplenty. We got to get 'em!"

"But how?" inquired another doubtfully. "We tried to get the old mammy and her little un. They busted the net. Later we thought we had the one that followed the *Bay-Rovers* into this bayou. He got away—an', b'gosh, he came nigh onto drowndin' us into the bargain!"

The burly fisherman who had first spoken clawed contemptuously at his scraggly beard. "Humph! Takes a bit o' headwork to do this trick. Leave it to me!"

"When'll we try to ketch 'em?" chorused several of the Pirate Islanders.

"Mullet schools are scarce now," explained the big fisherman. "The porpoises are huntin' 'em all about. Some mornin' about daybreak ye'll hear a big wanderin' school o' mullets skippin' up the Bay. The porpoises'll be after 'em. Then, you dumbbells, we'll be after them sea-hogs!"

PIRATE SCHEMERS

IT WAS true that the roe-fat mullet schools were now scarce. The run was over. Lawful fishermen no longer struck them with their nets, for this was the season, protected by law, when the millions of eggs hatched into baby mullet. It would be two months before the regular fishermen would work at their trade.

It was December. The storm season, too, was past. A clear azure sky hung constantly over the sparkling Bay. The *Palm Scout* steamed up the channel daily, facing scarcely more than a cool, bracing Gulf breeze. Even December was mild in Pirate

Bay, the winds gentle and the water not too cold.

Never had Plumpy been so fat. Never had he felt so merry and full of play.

Wasn't he almost as much the leader as old Black-Porp? Of course, the old herd-bull *did* still give the orders for feeding and roving the Bay waters. It was true, too, that he acted like a tyrant at times, reminding every porpoise that *he* was their battle-scarred old leader.

But Plumpy didn't mind. He swam right beside Black-Porp. Sometimes when the main herd was slow to respond to the stern signals of the herd-bull, it was Plumpy himself who circled in among them, prodding them along forcefully, though he acted quite merry about it.

Today the porpoises were rolling down the Bay, their dark rounded backs rising above the surface every few seconds. At about this same time certain human pirates were moving. They were crossing the Bay in their white-painted *Bay-Rovers*.

One of this crew suddenly jabbed a rough finger toward the distant porpoises. "There's what we want right now!"

"Huh," rasped another man. "Reckon we want 'em right now; but we cain't get at 'em out in the middle of the Bay."

The big fisherman with the scraggly beard had been studying the surrounding waters with cunning eyes. "Nope, not there and now; but I got a hunch a big school o' mullet will be passin' up Pirate Bay sometime before mornin'."

The rest of the crew chuckled with gloating delight. "If so, then us and the porpoise-hogs'll be there too!"

But Plumpy and his herd knew nothing about that. A familiar plume of smoke could be seen near Seagrape Island. It was the *Palm Scout*. The porpoise herd rolled on to meet it.

There were many passengers on Captain McKinley's steamboat today. They were winter tourists, going to the resort on Gulf Zephyrs Island.

As the porpoises appeared, rolling their fat black forms and *whoofing* into the air, the passengers laughed delightedly.

"Hey, Dad! Look at them turn somersaults!" exclaimed a boy at the rail.

"Black whizzes!" cried another young passenger admiringly. "If I could swim like that, I'd never want to stay on land!"

Just then Plumpy gave a boiling turn, and dived. A moment later he came up in the lead of the frolicking porpoises. The passengers could see the streak of pale gray, the lasting scar left by the octopus he had slain.

"The plumpest one," said a young man's voice, "seems to have had a sea fight." It was Warden Gregg speaking.

"Yes," agreed the captain, casting his keen eyes toward Plumpy, "but he doesn't seem to have been hurt much. The roe season has certainly made them all fat."

The warden looked thoughtfully up and down the long blue Bay. White gulls circled. Here and there a pelican glided. On a distant reef perched a flock of black cormorants. Pirate Bay seemed very peaceful.

"I guess," Warden Gregg decided presently, "the porpoises will be safe now. I'm going on to Gulf Zephyrs and rest a while.

I don't believe that Pirate Island seine-crew is moving around much now."

But on that point he was wrong!

PORPOISE OIL

THE big mullet school passed up Pirate Bay at dawn next morning. It was one of those occasional schools which run in great numbers, but spawn later than the others.

The porpoises, just emerging from a night's rest, sensed the telltale vibrations—the faint rumblings of thousands of small fish-fins.

Black-Porp shoved off at once. Plumpy, eager with excitement and hunger, was right beside the old leader. The herd followed willingly.

Far ahead the mullet school, leaping and weaving thickly in the water, moved steadily into the upper reaches of the Bay. They were making for Hurricane Pass, where they would enter the Gulf for more room to spawn.

And in the mouth of a creek a shivering fisherman suddenly detected the skipping commotion of the fast-moving school. He strained his eyes, looking beyond the school. Far in the distance he caught a faint glimpse of the porpoises as they rolled momentarily to the surface.

That was enough for him. He had been waiting several hours for what he now saw. With a silent chuckle, he quickly turned his skiff about, and poled rapidly back to camp.

"They pass!" he cried to the sleepy-eyed seiners. "A big school o' mullet—an' our porpoises are rollin' along not far behind!"

Sleepiness instantly vanished from the men's eyes. With exclamations of evil joy they rushed aboard the speedy white launch. Several skiffs, bearing large-meshed nets especially designed for big, fighting bodies, had already been tied to the *Bay-Rovers'* stern.

In stealthy haste the lawless crew began winding out of their hideaway. "Head-work, boys!" laughed the bearded man. "I told you it would happen. Them sea-hogs'll never bust out o' these nets. They're stout enough to hold ten-foot sharks!"

The weaving school of mullet hove to. Hard ahead lay the outlet of Hurricane Pass. Water rippled, swirled, spattered from their agitated movements. Almost upon the mullet came Plumpy and his hungry herd. They could feel the thrilling surge of a thousand little bodies just ahead. Now they could eat enough to keep them fat for another dozen tide-turns.

Suddenly the porpoises boiled up in the midst of the milling school of fish. And at that shrewdly-timed moment, several skiffs began to leap out from various hidden points ahead, un-reeling yards and yards of mullet-net, cutting off the mullet's escape through Hurricane Pass.

Two other skiffs, nearer by, rushed together from opposite points with the porpoise-seine. Most threatening of all, the white launch was suddenly roaring from behind. Out of her stern another porpoise seine was being unreeled, circling swiftly to join the nets ahead.

As delicious as Plumpy was finding the food he was so busily bolting down, his muscular body went suddenly tense. Distinctly he heard the dull, regular clanking of nets being paid out. He knew the sound of lead and cork lines reeling across a skiff's stern.

More sinister to his now suspicious instincts was the roar of the motor-launch, and the *blop-blop-blop-blop* noise made by the rapid unwinding of a kind of net entirely new to him. What was all this disturbance?

Plumpy swirled violently, signaling the others. Out of the water came his rounded head, eyes peering about with alarm. Boats seemed to be moving everywhere! Uttering an amazed *whooof* Plumpy dived, boiled warningly among the feeding porpoises.

But the old herd-bull, too, had discovered these menacing happenings all around them. He smashed the water with his tail, the sort of violent signal he seldom used. The seasoned leader knew instantly that complete extermination of his family was facing them! Something had to be done mighty fast!

Their huge meal of fish was entirely forgotten. Black-Porp, ordering his family as low as possible in the water, fled for safety. But he hadn't traveled a dozen yards before his alert eyes told him he had made a mistake. Dimly through the brightening water, he saw the menacing pattern of a gray-threaded net.

Without losing speed, Black-Porp swerved with his herd, and headed in boiling haste for the motorboat. That was the one lane of safety—to overtake that evil craft, to flash out of this trap ahead of it!

Unfortunately, the motorboat had too nearly completed its snarling circle.

Plumpy and his entire family were trapped!

A sensation more dreadful than ordinary fear throbbed in Black-Porp's experienced body. He realized instinctively that this was, at last, the strange fate he had somehow sensed in these recent months. Too many things had happened to his family. And from this final calamity not even his over-cautiousness had saved him. The fattening pleasures of the mullet-roe season had thrown him off guard.

The ominous man-activity had not halted. Of this Plumpy himself was aware. Boats continued to ply back and forth, rapidly.

The porpoises made an agitated circle about the net enclosure. But on all sides stretched an unbroken netline—stout, sagging folds whose meshes were just large enough to tangle fatally about their leathery flippers and tails if the porpoises fought it!

Black-Porp began to swirl back and forth, blowing furiously. The white motor-launch had eased across the grounded staff of one net. It began churning again. The end of the other net was caught up, and the motorboat was towing it yard by yard. Closer and closer the net was drawn—smaller and smaller grew the enclosure trapping the porpoises!

Not every porpoise could leap as Plumpy had in his earlier desperate plight. Besides, they were all too fat and heavy now for such water acrobatics. And to forestall just such a possibility, the rest of the skiffmen had hurriedly returned from dropping their nets around what they could of the fleeing mullet school.

All the skiffs were now strung out around the porpoise seine. The top line of the deep, sagging net was being raised from the water and hooked securely to the boats. In each skiff stood a fisherman, planted firmly on hefty legs; and in his hands each one grasped a wickedly sharp harpoon!

In a desperate blind rage, old Black-Porp charged the net. His fury set the whole herd to churning about in the water. Some of them collided with the deadly meshes, and soon the entire net was being yanked wildly.

The pilot of the motor-launch shouted hoarsely, "Get your

skiffs outa the way—you'll get sunk! We've got 'em tangled now; they cain't get away."

Frantically the fishermen fought with the net which was jerking their skiffs right and left. The net was slipped free, and the men moved back to gloat over the helplessly threshing porpoises.

Plumpy, remembering his past experiences, had managed to shy away from the meshes which now entangled his proud herd. But he felt so desperate that he continued to wallow violently around in the midst of the fighting mammals.

Again and again his octopus-scored back heaved and rolled without touching the net.

"Watch that one!" cried one of the men. "His scar shows he's been in other fights. Probably the toughest young bull of the whole herd. Get *him!*"

From three skiffs barbed harpoons came hurtling toward Plumpy's position in the middle of the wildly battling family. He was being singled out for the first kill!

THE CAPTAIN'S PREDICTION

IN a maddened blur of spuming water and threshing tails, Plumpy beheld those strange missiles slanting toward him, as deadly hostile as Indian arrows. He dived, with the power and swiftness of frenzy. He felt cool metal glance across his sleek side.

But none of the harpoon points found their mark. Fuming because of their poor marksmanship, the fishermen wound in the lines which held the evil prongs. They set themselves to throw again, the instant Plumpy's scarred back should reveal itself. But Plumpy did not immediately reappear. Instead he plowed into the net which was almost as dangerous. Quickly his twirling movements tangled him in the crisscrossed threads.

For many minutes the helpless porpoises battled on, fighting a shapeless monster they could never conquer. Even old Black-Porp, the veteran of many perilous encounters, seemed to recognize that grim fact.

Their combined struggling began to grow weaker. Some of the trapped creatures were so tangled they were unable to get their snouts above water long enough to breathe fresh air. Black-Porp, the aging herd-bull, was practically exhausted. Only at one point of the net did the battle rage on. That was where one yearling bull, showing blurred glimpses of a pale gray scar, continued to plunge and twist at the confining meshes. Plumpy was still undefeated!

The big bearded man, who had now moved the motor-launch in close, suddenly shouted an order: "Look aside, all of you! We've got to hurry this mess along before somebody comes snoopin' around here. Make way—this'll fix that mad young bull!"

The other Pirate Islanders made haste to clear out of their captain's range, for he now held in his hand, not a harpoon, but a high-powered rifle!

With careful aim at the one porpoise still fighting the net, the fisherman pulled the trigger. *Plunnnng-zoooooo!*

The bullet struck empty water, glanced, went whistling away.

Plumpy had accidentally plunged out of range. He didn't know what that whining thing was which had struck so close to him, but he knew it was hostile, threatening. Feeling his powerful body swelling with new fury, he reared.

But the rifleman had raised his weapon for the second time, and again his grimy finger was curling about the trigger.

Before he could shoot, one of his men spoke warningly, "Cap'n, maybe you shouldn't fire that rifle out here." He looked furtively around them. "Somebody'll hear that there gun, an'——"

"Well," glared the bearded gunman, "d'you want to hang out here all day until somebody *does* come along? Thing to do is to kill that crazy sea-hog before he gets the others fightin' again."

Almost as if the porpoises had all understood that excited rumble of talk, the entangled herd suddenly aroused themselves. Encouraged by Plumpy's tireless battling, old Black-Porp himself forced new spirit into his weary frame.

Once more a furious threshing of water set up a widespread turbulence. Every porpoise seemed to be buckling and plunging against the cruel net with even more fury than when they had first felt themselves surrounded. Plumpy's courage and unconquered strength had heartened them.

The mad struggle was deafening. The fishermen were now shouting angrily, both at the helpless porpoises and at one another.

The rifleman, however, had lowered his gun. "We'll let 'em quiet down once more," he told his men loudly. "Then we got to plug 'em all before——"

He never finished his remark. Hard by came the roar of motors growing louder by the second; and before the lawless fishermen were able to understand just what was happening, two speedboats appeared—one swerving around the side of the mangrove key, the other throbbing in from the opposite direction.

"The fish warden!" croaked the bearded rifleman. "Scatter!"

But Warden Gregg, assisted by deputies in both speedboats, was gliding up, sharp eyes alert to every move the lawbreakers might make.

"You'll stay just where you are!" came his stern command. The speedboats slowed to a standstill. The young warden cast an angry glance at the trapped porpoises, then eyed the fishermen contemptuously. The porpoises were exhausted.

"So you'd go to all this trouble for a few dollars' worth of blubber-oil! Kill out a Bay herd as friendly and intelligent as these porpoises!"

In the tense silence that followed, more splashings could be heard, the faint noises made by the mullet left in the nets close to the Pass.

"Catching mullet out of season, too, eh?" said the young warden. "Well, that means another charge against you." He smiled grimly. "I told Captain McKinley that I was going to rest a few days at Gulf Zephyrs. Instead, I'll spend the next few minutes arresting the whole lawless lot of you!"

At the warden's word, his deputies swung alongside the Bay-Rovers. Guns and harpoons were taken.

"Now then," ordered the warden, "you can spend the next half hour cutting the net away from these porpoises."

Sullenly the men set about the difficult work. Hardly had they touched the net before Plumpy was roused to a new frenzy, and led his cramped herd in another furious battle of plunges. The skiffs were rocked so violently that two of the fishermen were thrown overboard. They came up sputtering, half-strangled. But Warden Gregg and his deputies forced them to continue the task. Finally the net was slashed apart. The porpoises, wearied and scarcely realizing they were miraculously free, lolled about for a brief moment.

Plumpy sensed what had happened. As the net grew slack about his fat body, he gave a terrific thresh of his flat tail, and bolted down the Bay. The rest of the herd, with final *whoofs* of weariness, followed in his wake.

Behind the freed porpoises, Warden Gregg and his deputies hustled the Pirate Islanders toward Hurricane Pass. There he forced them to free whatever mullet were still alive. Then, confiscating their illegal nets, he set out with his prisoners for the mainland, where the law might take its just course.

For the remainder of that day Plumpy rested with his family in the still waters of a remote cove. Two days later, when the friendly herd boiled up as usual around the *Palm Scout*, not one of them appeared to be hurt.

True, Black-Porp seemed a little less active. Age was telling on that battle-scarred old herd-bull. But ahead of him today swam another male porpoise—a fat, sleek creature with a thin gray scar across his back and side.

That was Plumpy, and he had never rolled along so gracefully nor so proudly!

"See that one?" the captain asked a passenger. "Well, sir, in my opinion that porpoise has already been selected by his herd as their future leader. Why, that octopus mark along his side looks to me like a badge of honor!"

When the whistle blasted for Buttonwood Island, Plumpy turned his five-foot body around. Black-Porp followed at his flank, and the others hurried along eagerly. They knew that Plumpy would lead them to some delectable meal.

This Plumpy did, for already his senses, now amazingly keen, had traced unerringly a school of silver mullet. Presently, along the fishing flats of Pirate Island, he and his herd were feasting on delicious slabs of the sweet meat.